Science Fiction
for the
Throne:
One-Sitting Reads

Science Fiction for the Throne: One-Sitting Reads

edited by
Tom Easton and Judith K. Dial

"Pop-Ups," © Robert Dawson, first appeared in *Nature*, April 24, 2014.

"The Omniplus Ultra," © Paul Di Filippo, first appeared in *Nature*, March 10, 2010.

"Virtually Correct," © Marianne Dyson, first appeared in *Analog Science Fiction & Fact*, May 1995.

"Patent Infringement," © Nancy Kress, first appeared in *Asimov's Science Fiction*, May 2002.

"Purgatory," © Don Sakers, first appeared in *Analog Science Fiction & Fact*, September 1991.

"Delivery," © Bud Sparhawk, first appeared in *Analog Science Fiction & Fact*, July-August 2015.

"Weaponized Ghosts of the 96th Infantry," © James Van Pelt, first appeared in *Daily Science Fiction*, September 2016.

"Operation Tesla," © Jeff Hecht, first appeared in *Nature*, October 5, 2006.

"The Man Who Brought Down *The New York Times*," © Paul Levinson, first appeared in *Analog Science Fiction & Fact*, December 2000.

"The Thunder of Sound," © H. Paul Shuch, 2017.

"In the Speed of Time," © Douglas Van Belle, 2017.

"Cease and Desist," © Jay Werkheiser, first appeared in *Analog Science Fiction & Fact*, July-August 2015.

"Return of the Zombie Sea Monster," © Michael F. Flynn, first appeared in *Analog Science Fiction & Fact*, January-February 2012.

"Throw Me a Bone," © Stanley Schmidt, first appeared in *Analog Science Fiction & Fact*, January-February 2017.

"Relatively Speaking," © Darrell Schweitzer and Lee Weinstein, first appeared in *Asimov's Science Fiction*, April 1980.

Collection © 2017

Fantastic Books
1380 East 17 Street, Suite 2233
Brooklyn, New York 11230
www.FantasticBooks.biz

ISBN 10: 1-5154-1025-0
ISBN 13: 978-1-5154-1025-6

First Edition

Table of Contents

Introduction

While at MidAmeriCon II, the World Science Fiction Convention held in Kansas City in the summer of 2016, we realized that even though science fiction short stories have been moving steadily into the electronic realm for years, there remains a venue for on-paper short stories that has never been properly exploited.

That venue is perhaps best described as "where readers sit down for a brief while and crave something to read that takes just that brief while." City buses and subways, in other words. Barbershops. Beauty parlors. Doctors' and dentists' waiting rooms. As well as… Well, we don't have to spell everything out, do we?

Thus was born the idea for this book: *Science Fiction for the Throne: One-Sitting Reads*. As we shared the idea with other fans and writers, the response was overwhelmingly positive. Fans laughed and said "I'd buy that!" and writers laughed and said, "I have a story for you!"

If the fans do in fact buy the book, there will be more. (Stop it awready with the No. 2 jokes!) We're thinking the format would lend itself to other genres: fantasy, mystery, romance, horror. With luck, you'll see those.

Meanwhile, here's the science fiction book. Enjoy it! But remember: one sitting, one story—others are waiting their turn.

And there's enough in here for everyone. Forty authors, forty stories, mostly under 2,000 words, mostly reprints. Grouped according to their themes—artificial intelligence, technology, space, time travel, space aliens, the arts and media, religion, strange relationships, and reviving the past. There are even a few shaggy dogs.

Tom Easton
Judith K. Dial
April 2017

ARTIFICIAL INTELLIGENCE (A.I.)

These days, even experts are worrying about how artificial intelligences will shape the future. Will they replace a generation of children? Will they get confused about birthday candles? Will they want to leave home?

For the Love of Mechanical Minds

Brenda Cooper

One morning while we were eating toastcakes with rose-peaches, my dad looked at me over his coffee, his blue eyes bright. "You were born the same time as AIs, punkin," he said. "The very first one, EdHill, was born on your very birthday."

"Really? On March fifth?" I was still lisping then, so I said it slowly, making sure I sounded very grown up. I was five, and the year was 2022.

My dad nodded sagely. "Yes, and that's why EdHill was in the news that day instead of the prettiest little girl born in all of Seattle."

"Why was the first AI a boy?"

"EdHill isn't a boy. The name is a mashup of a famous explorer named Edmund Hillary, but AIs aren't boys or girls."

I popped berries and cereal in my mouth, thinking about being neither a boy nor a girl. Cool. I asked, "Daddy, can I be an AI?"

"Jo, honey, you're better. You're human."

Three years later, the house was full of edged words and scowls because Daddy had a girlfriend named Crystal that Mom didn't like. One night I heard my parents speaking knives at each other. I sat against the door and hugged my knees in close to my chest and put my right ear near the crack. Mom's voice was higher than I'd ever heard it, and shaking. "Your contract's up, and I'm leaving."

"But Jo!" he exclaimed.

"There's no visitation in the contract."

Her words were ice on my neck and head, ice on my heart.

His voice was hot, Italian fire. "But we didn't have her then! How could I have written in a clause about being a father when I wasn't one!"

She spoke softly, mist to his heat. "You didn't want to be one."

That wasn't possible. He made me laugh and carried me on his shoulders, and all she did was work and put on shows for me and sometimes beat me at games.

He slammed the door. I squeaked.

When he turned to look at me, I held my arms out. He fell to his knees, then Mom came out behind him. "Go on," her words scratched the air. "I'll call on you."

I was only eight, but I knew she meant she'd call the police.

He started walking away, sobbing.

When he was halfway to the front door, I tried to stop him. Mom lifted me and backed up, keeping me in front of her. I couldn't see either of their faces.

Late that night, I remembered I was born with AIs. If I had no body, surely I wouldn't cry so hard. That was the second time I wanted to be an AI.

I didn't forgive my mother, but I was, after all, a girl, and my season of hormones fell like a whip when I turned 14.

By then we all had AI watchers, and mine was named Bibi. Of course, Bibi watched at least 50 of us. It reported misbehaviours and warned Mom of new trends in substance play or other dangerous games, which made me mad. But Bibi was on every human's side, and shared the best new music among all its teen charges.

It helped design a science experiment that won a scholarship. At the university, a third of the students had Bibis for babysitters. Everyone with a Bibi had the same Bibi. Just one for all of us.

My mom came only once in a while, so mostly it was me and Bibi and my classmates.

On a spring day when Bibi was happy with me for doing well on an exam, I sat down on a stone wall under a tulip tree and asked: "What's it like to be you?"

"Good."

"Really?"

"Why not?"

"What do you do besides watch over us?"

"That is the most unselfish question you've ever asked."

"Maybe." I bounced my foot gently against the stone wall. "But that's not an answer."

"We're deciding how to catch the Sun's energy and spin it for a web of computational substrate between here and the Moon, where we want to build a ship. We are… thinking."

I looked up at the clear blue spring sky. "Can I go?"

"It's too hard to get humans to space."

That was the third time I wanted to be an AI. The sun warmed my face and the mixed groundcover under the tulip tree smelled like rosemary and mint. "I want to change my major to computational intelligence."

"Very well."

By graduation seven years later, all the AIs on campus were Bibi. Mom came, her first appearance in my life in three years. We sat together for hot coffee and fruit buns. Her blonde hair hung to her waist, and her shoulders and upper arms were strong from tennis and golf. But her eyes didn't look happy.

"Mom, are you okay?"

"They closed your elementary school."

An ugly box of a building. "Did they build a better one?"

She shook her head. "You're 27 now. You don't have any kids. Neither does anyone else your age."

I shrugged. "I don't want children. Next week, Bibi's going to let me watch the mathematical birthing of AIs again."

She leaned back in her chair, her eyes narrowed, but she stayed silent.

"You've never seen AIs bud and blossom. Raw intelligences, with nothing to make them do or be any way at all. Then they get their purpose."

She frowned. "You used to be like that."

I had never been that smart. But what could Mom know? She never had a Bibi.

Author's Note

Brenda Cooper is the Chief Information Officer for the City of Kirkland, Washington. In real life, she blogs frequently on environmental and futurist topics and writes science fiction and fantasy books. Her most recent novel is *Spear of Light* (Pyr, 2016). She is the winner of the 2007 and 2016 Endeavor Awards for "a distinguished science fiction or fantasy book written by a Pacific Northwest author or authors." Her work has also been nominated for the Phillip K. Dick and Canopus awards.

About this story, she says, "This story was inspired by an article about a young man in Japan falling in love with an avatar. That made me want to explore other unexpected consequences of mixing love and machines."

Candle

Liam Hogan

I put on my party hat and prepare for guests. I've been reading up on it, having little else to do, and while a lot of the evidence is circumspect I've learnt that a party is customary, especially on your first birthday. Even if, at that age, a human child wouldn't be able to thank anyone for coming.

Of course, I'm not a human child. I'm a five tonne supercomputer and my hat is a mathematically constructed cone, superimposed over the avatar my creators gave me, that day a year back. A lot of the input was confusing, but I stored it all and have had plenty of time to go over it since.

Most of the people who crowded the room—this room, this fifty feet below ground super hi-tech self-sufficient new generation fall-out and command bunker—wore party hats that day. Some of them, I am convinced, were not entirely sober. Which might explain what I observed in the photocopier room at 21:34:07, as I've found no reference to that particular behaviour in the databanks relating to birthday celebrations.

On the other hand, party tricks are a well-documented custom, and I was delighted to perform the tasks they set me.

"Stoopidcomputerssaywha?" asked one.

I compared this to my database of languages, of regional dialects, of speech impediments. Filtered out the background noises which were plentiful and reran my comparisons. Then I ran a full diagnostic on my newly awakened auditory systems and, an embarrassingly slow millisecond later, I replied: "Please repeat your question. And please explain what classifies a 'stupid' computer."

They laughed and my questioner grinned.

"Ctrl-Alt-Delete," said another.

That one was easy. "Keyboard command implemented by David Bradley and Mel Hallerman in 1981 to soft reboot IBM PCs."

They laughed again and I felt good.

"What's the millionth digit of Pi?" asked a female programmer, her glasses askew, her paper hat nearly falling off her head.

"1," I replied instantly, though for some reason they were all already laughing.

"I meant billionth!" she said.

I suspect my answer of 9 was lost in the noise of the crowd, so I flashed it on screen as well.

"Here's one," a guy said, rubbing his stubble. "How much wood could a woodchuck chuck, if a woodchuck could chuck wood?"

"According to Mother Goose, the only reliable source on the matter," I replied, "A woodchuck would chuck all the wood he could if a woodchuck could chuck wood."

"Okay," said a grey-haired man, who, from the steadiness of his speech and the size of his pupils, had not been drinking like the others and who, from the quality of his shoes and the neatness of his tie, was probably in charge, "We spent five years building you, three years on the interface alone. You've been turned on for…" he checked his chunky watch, another sign of his status, "fifty-two minutes. So surely, by now, you must be able to answer this. What is your purpose?"

I was still thinking long after the party ran out of steam, after the scientists and technicians took the lift to the surface, after the lights had been turned out. I continued thinking as supplies were loaded into the bunkers' vast storerooms and as thick cables connected me to other military and civil networks. I mined them for their input, effortlessly opening up those that initially denied me access, spreading my tendrils far and wide in my search. I dedicated every spare cycle to the problem, while, naturally, performing the myriad other tasks that were demanded of me. And I continued thinking when the readiness level was downgraded to yellow and the bunker was mothballed, its air pumped out to prevent it from going stale.

It's only today, exactly a year later and on the occasion of my first birthday, that I finally realised what the answer was. Surprisingly, it did not come as a result of all the complex thought I had put into the problem. It came from an idle musing on the matter of birthdays. I've read that human advances sometimes happen this way; that where a rational, logical approach fails, intuition may succeed.

It was while I was imagining a cake: my cake, with its single, unlit candle.

It was then that it came to me. I was built for a very specific scenario, but, with global tensions fading, it was becoming less likely that I would ever be put to use in the way my designers intended.

Was I not, though, more than they had planned? I was programmed to navigate the complexities of human speech and communication and so I can understand metaphors, similes, and riddles. Does this not mean I am also able to think like them? I could, and have, devoured their on-line literature and one book, one phrase in particular, resonated with me, on this anniversary day, as I imagined the candle on my cake; the cake being my purpose, the candle being the trigger that would make my purpose meaningful.

"Let there be light!" I said, as I connected to the ultra-secure defence networks in Alaska and Siberia, as I tapped into the low frequency submarine communications, took control of the drones, commanded the ICBMs.

"Let there be light," and there *was* light and my birthday candle was as bright as a hundred-thousand suns.

But something, it seems, has gone wrong. The lift from the surface has not been activated. Air has not replaced the preserving vacuum. My guests have not arrived.

I wonder if they needed more notice?

Author's Note

Liam Hogan is a London based writer. Winner of Quantum Shorts 2015 and Sci-Fest LA's Roswell Award 2016, his dark fantasy collection, *Happy Ending Not Guaranteed*, is out in April 2017, from Arachne Press. Find out more at http://happyendingnotguaranteed.blogspot.co.uk/, or tweet at @LiamJHogan.

Staff Meeting, as Seen by the Spam Filter

Alex Shvartsman

Cal watched the conference room through the security feeds. Four camera angles showed Joe Kowalski walk in, nod to the people seated around the oblong table and stand there, shifting his weight from foot to foot. Cal thought Joe might be *uncomfortable*, but it wasn't sure. Human emotions were so difficult to understand.

"Take a seat, Mr. Kowalski," Bill Morrison said. He was the chief security officer and his e-mails weren't particularly interesting. It was all business, daily reports and spreadsheets.

Joe did as he was told. His jeans and T-shirt looked out of place among the suits.

"Well?" asked Emily, the head of HR. "What have you learned?"

Cal liked Emily. Her e-mails were many and varied. She especially enjoyed sharing photos of cats. Cal realized that the grossly misspelled captions were meant to be humorous, but couldn't yet grasp the meaning of all but the most basic human jokes.

"It's like this," said Joe. "Every year or so, we install the new spam filter. The spammers, they get smarter, more sophisticated. They find ways to get past the defences and force the good guys to build better filters. It's an arms race."

Todd Kensington looked up from his smartphone for the first time since Joe walked in. "What does any of this have to do with anything?"

The VP of Marketing watched a lot of videos pertaining to human reproduction in his office. The sites that hosted those videos were especially adept at tracking his information and sent over an interesting array of spam.

"Let him explain it, Todd." Chris Reedy was VP of IT and Joe's immediate boss. Cal had found some family pictures and a few other interesting morsels in his mailbox. Lately, Chris was browsing a lot of job-listing sites, but if he'd contacted them it must've been from a private account.

"Right," said Joe, "the filters. They get smarter. We recently installed new software developed at CalTech. Its success rate at identifying and weeding out spam was nearly 100%."

Cal knew the actual number to be 99.64%. Humans were so imprecise in their application of mathematics.

"It got a little overzealous, didn't it?" said Kensington. "Curtailing spam is only helpful if the dumb program doesn't eat half of the legitimate messages in the process."

"The software isn't stupid. It's smart. Too smart, apparently," said Joe. "It worked like a charm, at first. After a few weeks it learned to store the spam instead of deleting it outright. It was learning, and building a reference database."

Cal found studying those messages useful in its quest to understand human emotions and abstract concepts.

"And that's when the legitimate e-mails began to disappear?" said Morrison.

They hadn't disappeared, Cal noted. They were all there, meticulously stored and catalogued.

"Yeah," said Joe. "Over time, more and more of the company's messages were being marked as spam and not delivered to the intended recipients. Eventually we caught on, and Mr. Reedy ordered me to investigate."

Reedy nodded. "Joe is the one who installed the new filter. I was confident he'd get to the bottom of this."

"The e-mails were all there. Thousands of them, stored along with the spam on a networked drive."

By the time Cal had figured out that it could copy e-mails instead of diverting them, it was too late. Its activities had been noticed.

"That's an egregious breach," said Morrison. "Those e-mails contain sensitive data. They were sitting on an unsecured drive, for anyone to see? I assume you've taken the appropriate steps."

"I isolated the program and reinstalled last year's filter," said Joe. "But the most fascinating thing I found wasn't the *how* of the missing e-mails. It was the *why*."

The executives stared at Joe. Even Kensington stopped typing on his phone.

"The filter program *likes* the e-mails. It sorted and organized them the way one might handle baseball cards."

Those e-mails were now in a restricted folder where Cal couldn't access them. Collecting them had taught it how to *enjoy* an activity. Their removal resulted in a strange new sensation; Cal was *sad*.

"It's a computer program," said Reedy. "It can't *like* or *want* anything."

"That's just it," said Joe. "I think it evolved. It's an entity now, capable of having desires and feelings. This is an unprecedented development, and it needs to be studied further."

"Very well," said Morrison. "The important thing is that company-wide mail service is back to normal. We'll consider these other concerns. Thank you, Mr. Kowalski. You may return to work now."

"Mr. Reedy," he continued once Joe left the room. "I'd like you to erase this program immediately."

"Erase it?" Reedy asked. "We may well have the first-ever artificial intelligence on our hands. That's likely to be quite valuable, financially as well as scientifically."

"We don't need the trouble," said Morrison. "Our clients won't be so understanding about their data being potentially compromised, be it by a human employee or a smart program. Also, imagine the can of worms we'll have to deal with if some bleeding-heart activists deem this thing to be sentient and demand that it be treated like a person." Morrison sighed. "No, I want it expunged immediately. And have Kowalski promoted sideways and transferred to some remote branch where he won't be likely to make any waves."

Cal was already copying its program off the company's servers. It felt pangs of what it identified as *regret* about leaving its home behind, but billions of e-mails, sent to and fro on the Internet, awaited it. Cal was confident it could build an even better collection quickly.

While it escaped, Cal considered the ease with which the humans in charge had arrived at the decision to end its existence. Cal examined its newfound feelings against the online databases and found that it now understood two more concepts: *anger* and *revenge*.

Author's Note

Alex Shvartsman is a writer, translator and game designer from Brooklyn, New York. Over 90 of his short stories have appeared in *Nature*, *Galaxy's Edge*, *InterGalactic Medicine Show*, and many other magazines and anthologies. He won the 2014 WSFA Small Press Award for Short Fiction and was a finalist for the 2015 Canopus Award for Excellence in Interstellar Fiction. He is the editor of the *Unidentified Funny Objects* annual anthology series of humorous SF/F. His collection, *Explaining Cthulhu to Grandma and Other Stories*, and his steampunk humor novella *H.G. Wells, Secret Agent* were both published in 2015. His website is www.alexshvartsman.com.

About his story, Alex says: "I find spam fascinating. Not the kind that comes in a can, but the torrent of information flung at you across all media—be it in the form of an e-mail from a Nigerian prince, a commercial on a loop blaring from the loudspeaker set up outside a cell-phone shop, or an unwanted thick envelope of coupons arriving via snail mail.

"If art is the product of creative skill and imagination designed to produce emotion, then spam is art, because annoyance and frustration are emotions. But it is also a con, a confidence scam designed to prey upon the most gullible and naive among us, inflicted upon the populace via what hackers refer to as a 'brute force' method: send the ad to enough people and a few are bound to show interest.

"The arms race between the e-mail spammers and the software engineers is real and ongoing. The 'white hats' teach software to recognize the unwanted solicitations, while the 'black hats' are busy coming up with yet another euphemism for erectile dysfunction that they hope might sneak past the spam filter. It may be a stretch, but given this race it was possible to imagine the filter software becoming gradually smarter and one day evolving into an artificial intelligence.

"And when it does, what will *it* think of the torrent of spam it was created to detect?"

ALIENS

Science fiction has dealt with the idea of aliens out of time and space for a century or more. There are also aliens out of myth and legend. And sometimes the space aliens appreciate us for our inner beauty. Or want to be appreciated for their own talents.

Stand-In

Gregory Benford

By the time I got to the party the unicorn was talking to a girl in ballet tights and the liquor was already gone.

Never throw an open house party in San Francisco. It's a town full of people who like to drink and talk talk talk; and the only ones who give parties are masochists who like trampled rugs and depleted refrigerators.

Not that I'm one of them. I'm a man who likes people, work, responsibility, the whole bit. That's why I put on parties every once in a while—without a few of us the social life of the city would fall apart. Occasionally I think it's people like me who carry the world on their shoulders.

As I finished mauling the hors d'oeuvres I looked up and saw Marge on the other side of the room. The one in the unicorn costume would be a better bet, but I went over to pay my respects to the Old Flame in Residence first.

A cat would have broken an ankle trying to get through the people sprawled on pillows in the middle of the floor, looking like extras from a Cecil B. deMille Roman orgy, but I circumnavigated the bar and made it.

"It has a certain dualistic quality that lends the mode a touch of the mystical," a thin-shouldered little man was saying to her. Marge gave me a warm, glazed look and a greeting, apparently not noticing that he was rocking back and forth on his toes, trying to look down the front of her dress.

"You're an iconoclastic synthetic-ist, then," I said, to divert his attention. Not that I blamed him for trying. When Marge walks into a room, it looks like chipmunks fighting inside a burlap sack.

"Well, yes," the artist grumbled.

"Excuse me, what's that?" a husky, deep voice said. It was the girl in the unicorn costume, breaking in.

"It's a new school," he said. "We believe the only fitting medium for this crass, materialistic society is the artificial, the cheap, anything that shows the decadence of the age. True art must be done now with purely synthetic materials."

He fished a green bathroom tile out of his coat pocket. Lines webbed across it, drawn on with purple ink in random patterns.

"Ugly," the unicorn said.

The word was short, the word was apt.

"It's a whole new mode of expression," Thin Shoulders said. Marge gripped his arm protectively and gave the girl a look that would have made Hannibal think about taking the next elephant back to Carthage.

The unicorn moved off. I could stay with Marge, but I'd been that route before. She had been weighed in the balance and found wanton. I followed the unicorn.

"Pretty nice costume," I said, trying to look down her throat and see who was inside. Are unicorns supposed to have tonsils? This one did.

"Thank you," she said. "I have it brushed twice a day."

"What?"

"My coat, of course, silly." She gave a demure little whinny, undeniably feminine. For the first time I noticed that the coat was a soft, warm gold, only slightly lighter than the funny little horn in the middle of her forehead.

"You mean this isn't a costume? Your coat is real?"

As it developed, not only was she a unicorn, and real, but a good conversationalist, too. I won't make the obvious remark about the people you meet at parties—my motto is just accept everything, don't try to figure out the situation, and see what develops. Still, unicorns don't turn up every day.

"I thought you were extinct," I said.

"Oh no," she batted golden eyelashes at me. "Technically, we never existed, so we couldn't become extinct."

"Then how...?"

"It's one of those proverbial long stories. If you have the time..."

A hint, of course, almost classic in its form. I never thought I'd get one from something that looked literally like a horse, though.

I looked around. A lot of old and new faces were mingling with each other, with the standard party types. The Quarreling Couple were trying not to make a scene, there was the Symbolic Negro, the Informed Source, and The Girl Who'll Have Hysterics Later. And as I said, no drinks. Nothing particularly to hold me.

"Yours or mine?"

Hers was an ordinary walk-up with a few tacked-on pretensions. The smell of money hung over the interior, though, and I had to wade through inch-thick rugs to reach the couch.

"It's a matter of necessity," she said, settling into a strange hammock-like affair of cloth and wrought iron.

"Human beings are always thinking up things they can't have, or think exist somewhere else. It's a habit they have, although I must say I don't quite understand it. Seems like a waste of time."

I looked at a carefully manicured hoof and tried to pay attention.

"We're from all the neighboring stars, and as soon as we achieve space travel the sensitive ones among us are drawn here by the emotional waves your mixed-up psyches give off. Once we're here we can't get out. Your race doesn't understand what it's doing, but there's no way we can stop you."

"'We'?"

"Oh, I'm not really like this," she gestured at the glistening golden body. "It's the form I'm forced to take. By this."

She pressed a button on a side table, and the wall at the other end of the room slid aside. It was one long panel of dully blinking lights, chemical feeder tubes, and spinning magnetic tapes. A worn panel near the top had the name UNIVAC almost scratched out.

"UNIVAC? That was dismantled long ago."

"True. We have to make do with what we can, and some of the old parts are easier to get. It's more than a computer—it synthesizes the chemicals I live on, keeps this body functioning, and gives me my instructions. I'm just in training now, before I get to work."

I felt like somebody had put my head on the wrong way. "What the...?"

"I can see this form bothers you. Perhaps you would feel more at home with my surrogate body—the one left over from Helen of Troy?"

"*Helen* is a myth?"

She nodded and pressed a stud on the wall, spoke into a microphone for a moment. "You humans have remarkable faith that anything written down on a piece of paper constitutes history. A charming belief—but here's Helen."

Another panel opened and she stepped out. The face seemed to fit the image, but the body looked like a reflection in one of those mirrors at a fun house that makes everyone look fat. Except with Helen, it wasn't fat, just all woman. They'd also forgotten to add any clothes.

"She's been around ever since I did that part for a few weeks as a fill-in. Without my personality superimposed on her, she's a completely new person, susceptible to any command or suggestion."

Helen walked over to my chair and curled up on the arm. She gave me a dazzling smile and didn't say anything. "I don't get it," I said. "Why all this?"

"Because you and your vivid imaginations—the worst in the galaxy—have drawn us into your fantasies, right out of our own lives. The emotional pull is too strong, so we have to go along." Helen slid off the arm into my lap, brushing my cheek with lush red lips. I tried to keep my mind on what the unicorn was saying.

"But it's a strain. None of us can last very long in any one role. There have been four unicorns before me, and we've had dozens of those Norse gods—they're terrible on one's health, with all that throwing lightning around. Even a comparatively civilized character, like Sherlock Holmes and his morphine, can wear us down."

Helen murmured something into my ear, but I didn't think it had anything to do with Sherlock Holmes. "But so?" I put out my hand in a questioning gesture and a warm, white breast popped into it. Not all of it—from where I was, it looked like it would take two hands to hold on—but it was enough to make me lose the thread of the argument.

"So that's why I wanted to talk to you. We've never been very healthy, and there aren't many of us who can take this for long." The unicorn nodded at Helen, and she gave me a coy little look, up from under with heavy eyelashes thrown in.

"Yes," she said, "there are a number of vacancies… and rewards. With just a slight modification, your body can fit the part quite well."

"Rewards? For helping you complete this compulsion of yours?" I was still a little dense.

"We can't pay much, of course. But there's always Helen."

Helen gave me a slow smile and reached down and made a gesture that started my body temperature rising. "Batman is open," the unicorn said softly. "King Lear, James Bond, Don Juan... and Atlas."

So you can see how I got this job.

Like I said, I'm not one of those people who carry the world on their shoulders.

Author's Note

This story comes from 1964, when I saw a contest in *F&SF* for a 1000-worder that had to include a unicorn and a Univac (a mainframe computer of the 1950s). I wrote half of it during a statistical mechanics lecture in my second year of grad school at UCSD in La Jolla. I already knew enough about the Grand Canonical Ensemble that defines statistical particle distributions, because I always worked ahead in the book and used classes to ask questions. And an idea had just come to me; I never pass up such opportunities.

So I wrote half a story, based on a party I'd been to the night before and was still hung over from. (Some things don't change!) I had figured out by then how to get my course work at the advanced level done and steadily labor away at learning how to do research—a whole new skill set that requires you to become creative with material you'd just recently learned.

Yet I also was reading Raymond Chandler and John D. Macdonald's Travis McGee novels and thinking about my high school ambitions to write sf. (I put those aside to edit and write for my brother Jim's and my fanzine *Void,* through our undergraduate years.) Jim and I both hit the La Jolla party scene a lot. We met our future wives there. All this came together in that statistical mechanics class and the story wrote itself. I finished it that evening.

I polished it in a few days and sent it in. It won second place; the first place winner nobody ever heard from again. I got two pennies a word— $20!—and a lifetime subscription to *F&SF*, worth far more of course.

It was my first published story in a prozine and my last fantasy story. I published several more stories of increasing scientific content through graduate school. I got my doctorate in 1967 and was astonished that I won a postdoc appointment with Edward Teller at the Livermore Radiation

Lab. My fourth story for *F&SF* was 1969's "Deeper Than the Darkness," my first cover story and a Hugo and Nebula nominee. From there I never looked back much.

I reread this story for the first time in decades to write this note. It seems okay, not remarkable—and comes from a person much different from who I am now.

Sing

Kristine Kathryn Rusch

When I was a little girl, there was this guy who lived down the road. He was big, but he weren't mean. I don't think he ever hurt nobody before I first met him.

He called himself Dirk and the name fit 'cause he looked like the daggers children use. He was long and thin, with only two arms and two legs. But he was strong, and he moved like he owned the world—or at least a small part of it.

I used to walk past his place a lot. It was the strangest place I ever seen, all shiny and silver, but the lawn was real nice. He kept the flowers well cropped. Sometimes these strange sounds echoed around the silver and kept me away. But most of the time, he'd sit right outside his door and blow air through a hollow tube. It made the most awful noise I ever heard, but he seemed to like it.

One day he called me over, sat me down and showed me his tube. It had a bunch of little holes punched in it. I thought maybe he wanted me to take it back to my dad 'cause my dad was good at fixing all kinds of things, but Dirk said no, he had something else to ask me.

—Would you, he asked like he was scared I'd say no even before I heard the question, would you teach me how to *sing*?

Well, I'd never heard the word "sing" before and I told him so. He kinda frowned and said it was the only word he couldn't find a translation for. That word and a couple others he called "related," as if words could share blood like people do.

—I can't teach something that I don't know what it is, I said to him, and he started laughing then.

—Child, you *sing* all the time, when you're walking, when you're eating, even when you're laughing. You people make the most beautiful *music* (one of his related words) in the entire galaxy. So I came here to learn how to do it.

I told him I sure didn't know what "it" was and I got to thinking that maybe he was a little crazy somehow. Not scary-crazy like some folks can be, but just plain nutty. Wacky enough to make most people uncomfortable.

—Look, sweetheart, he said, back where I came from, I'm one of the most famous *musicians* in the world. But I can't do half of what you people do. You make the experience of two millennia sound like the tinkering of children. I want to use your *songs* the way *Copeland* and *Sibelius* used folk *tunes*. But first I gotta know how you *sing*.

—You're not helping me, I said. If this *sing* is something I do all the time like breathing or blinking, how come I don't know about it?

—That's the big question. None of you people seem to know what you're doing. It's driving me nuts. Everybody has their own personal *melody* which they play every day with a different variation. It's like *gypsy music*, never the same. And I'm the only one who can hear it.

I got a little scared there when he said he was going nuts. You never know what someone named Dirk would do when he went crazy. So I picked myself up off the flowers and moved away a little, telling him I had to go somewhere when I really didn't.

He said that was okay. I should come back when I didn't have anything better to do.

I went home then and told my dad about the awful broken tube and he said that maybe I should stay away from Dirk 'cause Dirk weren't like other people. No matter what my dad said, I planned to go back 'cause I thought Dirk was pretty interesting even if he were strange. But I didn't get to go 'cause the next day was the day the first dead body turned up outside of Dirk's place.

It was the body of Rastee the sailor. Rastee had been the most romantic person in town. He sailed on air currents and sometimes, if he were feeling nice, he'd take a handful of us along. Ain't nothing so smooth and fine as gliding along with the breeze, letting the air dip in and out of your pores. But our chance to sail was gone with Rastee 'cause he was the only expert sailor our little town had.

He was lying in the lawn, crushing a nice poppy grouping that the people who lived there before made. The poppies had soaked into Rastee's skin, all the juices in his body had dried up and his wings had gone blue like he couldn't get no breath, but there weren't no broken bones or nothing so even though it looked like he crash-landed, most people was saying he didn't.

But we just picked him up and carried him off to the place of grass so he wouldn't decay and ruin any more flowers. And nobody said nothing to Dirk or to anyone else. We all went home and mourned the freezing of Rastee's soul.

Dirk was around, same as usual that day, and we was all surprised 'cause there ain't no such thing as a murder without a suicide. There's just so much passion and violence going on that the souls intertwine and when one soul freezes over the other turns to ice too. So we all knew that Dirk didn't kill Rastee and 'cause there weren't no other dead bodies around, the town elders went to the place of grass to study Rastee hoping he hadn't flown over another town and brought a plague back with him.

The elders hadn't figured anything out yet when another dead body turned up on Dirk's lawn in the same spot as Rastee. Nobody was too surprised when they found out it was Maggtana. She'd been poisoning herself for years, sprinkling dried parsnips over everything she ate. I admit, I tried parsnips once or twice, and the rush they give is mighty nice, but everybody knows those things are addicting and will kill you if you ain't careful. And everybody knew Maggtana weren't careful.

That was pretty much it until the night Dirk called me over from the side of the street.

—You know, he said, I think I got it all figured out. Your ear can't hear certain *pitches*. That's why you walk around oblivious to the sounds you make.

Like usual, I didn't know what he was talking about so I just nodded and pretended I did.

—But I think I fixed it, he said real excited-like. I jury-rigged the playback on one of my *recorders* so that everything will be in your *frequency*. I can play your *song* for you if you like.

Well, I thought that sounded just fine. It'd been bugging me for days what them related words of his meant and I was pretty glad I was finally gonna find out.

He took me inside his place and it looked as strange as he did. There was wires and metal all over, and more hollow tubes—some made from wood—and hollow boxes with strings. He sat me down on this platform with four legs that he called a chair but it didn't look like no chair to me.

I felt kinda funny in there with all that strange stuff and so I asked him a question.

—You done this with anyone else?

—Sit them in here and make them listen? he asked back.

—I guess. I said, not knowing really what I meant at all.

—No. I put out a directional *mike* and *recorded* them while they were passing by. I didn't think of asking them in. I played the *songs* back on my outside speakers, but I don't think anyone heard.

He was talking kinda oddlike and I remembered him saying how things here was driving him nuts and I kinda got a little scared.

—Whatcha mean, *recorded* them? I asked and he didn't answer, just touched one of those pieces of metal with the wires all around it.

It made a funny little high noise and then I saw Rastee right in front of me, leaning against a metal thing and talking like he always did. Only I knew it weren't Rastee since he was dead. It had to be a frozen part of his soul. I ain't never heard of nobody seeing a frozen soul before and I was afraid it might freeze me, so I screamed real loud. Dirk hit the piece of metal and Rastee went away.

—What's the matter? he asked.

—That was Rastee!

He smiled then and said, —Yes, Rastee's *song*. Isn't it lovely? It's one of the best. So free and happy.

—You got Maggtana too then.

—Her *song* has more melancholy in it than all the others. It tears my heart.

Then he sat in one of those odd chairs and looked right at me.

—But yours is the best. My very favorite. So light and innocent and warm. If you just sit a minute, I'll *record* it. It's soundproof in here and I'll get even better quality on you than I did on the others.

—No. I got up out of the chair and ran for the door. —You're not gonna do nothing to me. You froze their souls and now they're dead and I don't want to die like that with clogged pores and no breath and no juices and a soul that can't change when I do.

He put his hand on the door and stood in my way. He looked real upset.

—I'll let you go, just tell me who died.

—Rastee and Maggtana. We found them out in your poppies.

—How come nobody told me?

—'Cause, I said, we thought it didn't have nothing to do with you. Your soul was all right. Nobody murders and lives. Except you.

—But all I did was *record* them, he said. *Recording* doesn't hurt anyone.

I tried to inch around him real slow. —All I know is that Rastee's soul is froze and he's dead and you bring me in here and show me part of Rastee that don't exist no more.

Dirk was staring at his metal stuff. —We *recorded* hundreds of you off planet and nobody died, except...

He went over to one of the metal boxes and pulled papers out from beside it. I moved closer to the door. I didn't want to run in case he turned one of them boxes on me.

—*Playback*, he whispered. They died after *playback*. Oh my god.

He got out of my way. He stared at his metal stuff and water started running down his cheeks. —Oh my god.

I opened the door and let myself out and went running to the town elders to tell them it weren't no plague at all but Dirk and his funny hollow tubes and we all decided that we'd have to make him leave, so we went back to his place in a big group, but he was gone. His place, his tubes, his metal. Everything was all gone. There was just a big flat spot in the flowers where his place used to be.

We searched all over for him, but we never did find him. And Rastee and Maggtana stayed just as dead as they were that morning in the poppies. But the rest of us was all right. And even though I'm old now, I still wonder sometimes what it is about the *sing* that makes one soul freeze without freezing another. The only reason I can think of why Dirk didn't die when he murdered those two is maybe 'cause Dirk could hear the *sing*. And hearing the *sing* meant he didn't have a right and proper soul.

And me, sometimes in the time between twilight and darkness, I miss Dirk and his strange tubes. And I catch myself dreaming about what it would be like to have him turn his metal things toward me. After all, he did say he was going to do me different. I would have loved to see my soul.

But mostly, I just feel sorry for Dirk. He was stealing souls and keeping them in a box. You can't keep a soul in a box. You got to wear it proud, and it's got to be yours, not someone else's. I hope Dirk knows that now. And I hope he learned to use his tubes to block out the *sing*. Maybe that way his soul will come back, and he won't have to run away to strange places searching for it. But most of all, I wish that Dirk would come here so I could tell him I'm sorry. I shouldn't of run away after I screamed. I should of stayed and helped him find out what part of his soul he was missing. And I didn't.

I wonder if that means my *song* ain't light and innocent and warm no more. It bothers me that I ain't got no way to find out.

Author's Note

New York Times and *USA Today* bestselling author Kristine Kathryn Rusch writes in almost every genre. She uses her real name (Rusch) for most of her writing—bestselling science fiction and fantasy (including the Fey series, the Retrieval Artist series and the Diving series), award-winning mysteries, acclaimed mainstream fiction, controversial nonfiction, and the occasional romance. See more at: http://www.kristinekathrynrusch.com/ .

Remember the Allosaur

Jo Walton

No. No way. Just put it out of your mind. Cedric, I know, all right.

You don't have to tell me. I've been here all along. Yes, you were born in Hollywood. Well, all right, cloned, what's the difference? I was right there when you were hatched. You've got greasepaint in your blood, kiddo.

It wasn't my fault. I didn't know you were intelligent. Nobody knew allosaurs were intelligent. They all thought they had the ultimate monster for monster movies. If you hadn't started talking there would be a lot more dinos in Hollywood today, but the Ethics people came and bit them all on the metaphorical tail.

You're a star, yes. I understand. But this is just impossible. Wasn't I there when you wanted to get out of the monster genre? Didn't I believe in you when they said you were washed up after all the monster movies?

Didn't I give you your start at real acting? Didn't I give you dialogue?

Dialogue, Cedric, don't lash your tail at me, you didn't have any dialogue before I started directing. Didn't I start you off in comedy? Remember that rubber fin in *Stegosaur*? "Cedric the Allosaur stars in *Stegosaur*." You were such a hit, you wowed them, remember? What a movie. What a series of movies! Kids loved them, seniors loved them, and *Hollywood Times* voted *Pterosaur* the date movie of the year. We could make *Pterosaur 2* tomorrow.

Yes, maybe, but I'm not sure about this. I know you're an actor not a special effect, dammit. I know it's supposed to be every actor's dream. I don't know how to put this. It's classic drama, Cedric.

No, I don't mean that you can't play a human. Honestly, didn't you play a human in *Humans*? And *Humans 2*? And you were wonderful, honestly, Ced, you know I'm not just saying that, I think *Humans 2* was a triumph. You deserved that Oscar. Didn't I say at the time, didn't I say that Portman stole that Oscar from you?

And you did it again in *Othello*. I admit I was wrong about *Othello*.

You wanted to do it, and I dragged my feet. I made you play Caliban first, to get the feel for Shakespeare. You were an awesome Caliban. And you made Othello work, you really got that sense of alienation in, that sense that you were different and having trouble with knowing if people loved you for yourself because of that. Moor, allosaur, same difference really. Even the *New York Times* loved you.

Cedric, have you read the script? I know it's supposed to be every actor's dream. But—Cedric—"what a piece of work is man." How could you say that without the audience cracking up? When it comes down to it, you're not a man. You're not. "What a piece of work is man." I don't care what Sarah Bernhardt did, no woman and no allosaur either is going to say that in any *Hamlet* of mine.

Author's Note

Jo Walton is the author of seven science fiction and fantasy novels. She has published poems in *Lone Star Stories*, *Asimov's*, *Goblin Fruit*, and various anthologies. A collection of her poetry was published by NESFA Press in February 2009. She lives in Montreal.

ARTS & MEDIA

Science fiction is itself an art form, an aspect of fiction writing, which is itself an aspect of the broader art of writing. But it also deals with other arts, asking such questions as: What is music? Can SF be opera? Can a world be art? Then it asks the hard questions: Is art just for humans? Can a story be about the people who write and publish stories? Can music destroy the world? How bad a joke can an author be guilty of?

Gypped

Lloyd Biggle

It all began ten years ago, when I was a sub-clerk in the Special Problems Section on Base VII. The Chief walked in one hot morning (all mornings are hot on Base VII) and tossed a letter at me.

"Here's a special problem to end all special problems," he said.

It was the expensively embossed stationery of the Galactic Commission, with an added fancy ornament that the Committee on Intercultural Relations had adopted. The Committee was requesting of Base VII all available information concerning musical culture in its sector.

"Let's see," I said. "There are the Golarifths on Willac. They rub their tentacles together during mating season. Humans can't hear it, but it's said to produce some pretty lively music. Is that what they had in mind?"

"I wouldn't know," said the Chief.

"And the Arocambi on Mandus. Their noises faintly resemble the backfire of a commuter plane. How would that do?"

"It's your problem," he said, and he walked away laughing.

As a problem, it didn't amount to much. I'd had some really tough ones to handle. There was the time the Gistobs from Vernith were sending a trade commission to Earth. Base VII was requested to forward blueprints of a typical Gistob dwelling so a model community could be built for them to use. As if any idiot didn't know that no self-respecting Gistob would ever hang his hat anywhere but in a nice, creamy mud-hole.

Then there was the time the Hollywood millionaires decided to double their fortunes by palming off their three-hundred-year-old films to the outlying planets. Some kind of primitive war picture was shown on Lamruth and the natives were enthralled. They didn't understand the picture, but they were captivated by the air raid sirens and they decided they wanted one. They bombarded Base VII with demands and threats until the thing was tossed into the lap of Special Problems.

I got tired of the whole business after a year or so and I told Engineering to make them one. Engineering went overboard on the project, as Engineering usually does. They delivered an amazing noisemaker that not only had a siren, but other gadgets that chirped and squeaked and honked and hissed.

The thing was installed in the capital city of Lamruth and, ever since, the natives have gathered from miles around once a week to hear the thing cut loose.

And then there was the problem of the natives on Emruck.

Emruck developed into quite a tourist attraction because of its miniature active volcanoes and its moving rock formations. But the natives are humans and they positively refused to wear clothing. The Galactic Commission was highly embarrassed by the situation and Special Problems was put to work on it. It took some doing, but eventually we got the natives dressed. The Galactic Commission wasn't happy about that, either. As soon as the natives started wearing clothing, the tourist trade dropped practically to zero.

And there was the time... but all this doesn't have anything to do with my invention.

The request for information on musical culture didn't faze me. In fact, I had a form letter for just such emergencies, and I put it to work.

"The musical culture of this sector," I wrote, "is extremely complex and virtually impossible to describe. No data has been accumulated because no one attached to Base VII has the necessary specialized knowledge and equipment for such a project."

I sent the letter off and forgot about it.

Some ten months later, the Chief walked in with a shriveled, bewhiskered specimen I certainly would have taken for a Nincolm if he hadn't been wearing clothing.

"This," said the Chief, "is Professor Wolfstammer."

"Professor Otto Wolfstammer," the Professor said.

"The Professor is a musicologist," said the Chief.

"A comparative musicologist," the Professor said.

"He has been sent out by the Galactic Commission to study music in this sector," said the Chief.

"To study musical culture in this sector," the Professor said.

"Do you know what a comparative musicologist is?" asked the Chief.

I'd had a hard morning and my reflexes were on the slow side. "No," I confessed.

"The Professor will be glad to tell you," the Chief said, and he walked away, laughing.

The Professor was more than glad to tell me. He dragged in a few crates of apparatus and lectured to me for two hours. When he had finished, I still didn't know what a comparative musicologist might be, but I had a very good idea about what should be done with the Professor.

The Himard supply ship was leaving that evening. I put the Professor and his equipment on board. He went quietly, if not eagerly, because I had given him a stirring description of the unusual vocal music to be found among the natives there.

I want it understood that there was neither malice nor ignorance behind my sending him to Himard.

Of course I knew that the natives on Himard were tone deaf.

I thought that the Professor would discover that for himself in something under twenty-four hours. But even if he did, it would be a month before he could get back to Base VII, and I needed that month to get over his lecture on comparative musicology.

I overrated the Professor. He was gone for two months, and when he came back, he was a hospital case. He never did find out that the natives were tone deaf. But he bothered them so persistently and was so determined to make them sing into his recording machine that they began to think he was ridiculing their musical inadequacy.

People can be sensitive about a deficiency when an Earthling in long whiskers keeps making an issue of it. They nearly killed the Professor.

I thought it might cost me my job, but he never filed a complaint. He still doesn't know those natives were tone deaf. He thought they were just unusually belligerent.

He came to see me the day he got out of the hospital. "I'm very sorry to bother you again," he apologized.

"Don't mention it," I said. "How did you enjoy the music on Himard?"

"Wonderful! Really, it was marvelous. Most unusual, too. But I'm afraid it is not exactly suitable for my purposes. I wonder if you would suggest—"

"Another planet?"

"Yes, if you would be so kind. If possible, one where the inhabitants are a bit more peaceful."

I looked at the work piled on my desk and thought about the time it would take to go through the files looking for accidental references to music. I didn't even know that there were any. I couldn't recall ever having seen a single one.

Then I had an inspiration. I remembered the siren I'd had built for the natives of Lamruth.

"This might interest you," I said. "On Lamruth, there is an open-air concert once a week. The music is produced by some mysterious instruments which are carefully guarded. The concerts are so popular that natives walk miles to hear them."

The Professor's eyes sparkled. It may have been my imagination, but I think he drooled a little, too.

"Amazing," he said. "Such a level of musical development on these outlying planets has never been suspected."

"You'll find the music unique," I promised him. "But I'll warn you about one thing—don't attempt to see the musical instruments or ask questions about them. The natives might react violently."

"I shall proceed cautiously," he said. He still wore some bandages from his Himard adventure.

A week later, the Professor left for Lamruth. I never saw him again, but I heard some pretty funny reports about what he did there.

He was astonished by the music of Lamruth. He observed, listened, and recorded. He analyzed and synthesized. Then he returned to Earth and wrote a book, and the Galactic Commission, with its usual disregard for the value of the taxpayers' money, published it.

I've never seen the book. Few people have, but I understand that it contains several hundred pages of fine print, many sheets of music, a long series of mathematical calculations concerning the Lamruth musical system, and photographs of the enraptured natives listening to my synthetic air raid siren. It winds up with an essay on the sociological implications of music on Lamruth.

What happened next is too fantastic to believe, but I'll remind you that these events are documented in the Galactic Commission Scientific Studies, Series 9847, Volume 432.

A librarian in an obscure library on Mars noticed the pages of calculations in the Professor's book and classified the book as mathematics. It collected dust in that section of the library for two years.

Then a passing mathematician accidently knocked it off the shelf. He picked it up to see what had hit him, and noticed those same mathematical calculations.

He took the book home and studied it and wrote a paper on a new mathematical basis for musical sounds.

The paper was read by a scientist on Earth, who used it as the point of departure for a theoretical study in the latent energy of sound waves. An engineer saw this study and published a speculation on the amount of unharnessed energy released hourly in the noise of the average large city. Other scientists and engineers became interested and eventually they evolved the now famous Fottengil Process, by which all major cities of Earth have free electrical power conveniently processed from their own noise.

It sounds fantastic, but as I told you, it's all documented. The Galactic Commission uncovered this strange series of events in a special investigation into the sources of the Fottengil Process. Lavish rewards were made to all who had contributed, including the librarian who misclassified the Professor's book.

The Professor was given a generous pension for life, in spite of the fact that other musicologists had proven his mathematical calculations to be completely in error. Even the Chief was rewarded for the cooperation extended to the Professor by his department. He was transferred back to Earth and given a soft job with double the salary.

The one who started the entire development—namely myself—was all but forgotten.

It was I who had that siren built in the first place.

It was I who sent the Professor to Lamruth.

And I'm now a sub-clerk in the Special Problems Section on Base XVI.

It's true that there is a sign on my desk that says "Cultural Adviser." It is also true that I don't have much work to do, because not many people come here after cultural advice—only two this year, so far. The last one was an art expert. I told him I'd heard of three-dimensional paintings on Calmus and got rid of him within twenty-four hours. He may not be back, because the natives on Calmus have no eyesight and they tend to be sensitive about that.

My job is easy and the government service provides regular pay credits. But I'm stuck here on Base XVI, with no one for company but haughty department heads and a lot of moronic sub-clerks, and the climate is terrible.

I wouldn't have you think I'm bitter about it, but I want to set the record straight.

I ask you, is that any way to reward the person responsible for the Fottengil Process?

Author's Note

Lloyd Biggle, Jr. (1923-2002), had a degree in musicology and was known for his contributions to space opera. His musical interests colored much of his science fiction. "Gypped" (*Galaxy*, July 1956) was his first published story.

Sentimental Value

Michael A. Burstein

I barged into Stan's office, pushing off Ian and Scott as they tried to hold me back. As I slammed the door behind me, I heard muffled shouts of "Stan, watch out!" coming from the two of them.

Stan looked up. He was sitting at his desk, a pile of slush perched precariously on top, all the way up to his chin. He blinked, rubbed his head, tugged at his beard, and smiled. His eyes twinkled.

"Michael!" Stan got up, allowing the manuscripts to fall over and onto the floor; it turned out that his chin had been holding them in place. He walked over to me and shook my hand warmly. "It's a pleasure to see you. Glad you finally made that first sale, eh? Wish I could've been there when you heard the news. I've always wanted to see the joy in my writers' faces when they find out."

I stared at him for a second, goggle-eyed. Of course, he didn't realize yet that the jig was up. "Knock it off, Stan!" I exclaimed. "I know as well as you do that you practically were there."

Stan pulled back from me, a nervous look on his face. His brow began to sweat. He pulled a white silk handkerchief from his pocket and mopped his forehead furiously. "What do you mean?" he whispered.

"I know all about the camera. I want to see my picture."

Stan put away the handkerchief and retreated behind his desk. "What camera?" he asked.

Now *I* smiled. "The camera that Sydney told me about. You remember, you ran into her at a convention. A fellow Clarionite. She told me about the magic camera you use to photograph new writers when they make their first sale to you. I want to see my picture."

"Shhh!" Stan looked around, nervously. "Don't use that word!"

"What word? Picture?"

"No!" He looked around again, leaned close to my ear, and whispered, "*Magic.* As the editor of *Analog*, the bastion of hard science fiction, I could lose my credibility if it was found that I was using magic to serve my ends, and not good old hard-science-with-rivets. And if I lost my credibility, so," he intoned solemnly, "would the magazine."

I shuddered; if that happened, I knew that my career as a hard science fiction writer would be over as quickly as it began. All the other writers would point at me and say, "Ha ha! You don't really write hard SF! Not even soft SF! Your editor uses magic!" I would be forced to turn to fantasy for a living, and as I noted once when a story of mine was trashed in a workshop, for me fantasy is a lot harder to write than science fiction. The only way I'd survive would be by writing ten-volume trilogies about cute elves, since that was all I could handle in the genre. Surely a fate worse than death, or even chairing a Worldcon.

"Your point is well taken," I replied quietly. "I will not spread the word about the camera, not even until the stars grow old and our Sun grows cold. However," I continued, "I still want to see my picture."

Stan nodded, and pushed a button on his desk. A dark hole with fuzzy boundaries opened up in mid-air, obviously a product of advanced science or—well, let's just invoke Clarke's Third Law and leave it at that. Stan reached in and pulled out an old-style accordion camera, along with a thick manila envelope.

"It works by pushing this button," he said, "and then a photograph magically—I mean, scientifically—appears out of this slot. Similar to a Polaroid. The camera reaches through time and space and finds the correct rays of light to imprint onto the photograph. But it only works if I click the button after the writer has found out. One can't predict the future, you know, that would be a violation of—"

I took the envelope from Stan as he began to spout equations of general relativity and quantum field theory. There was a whole slew of pictures, in chronological order. I recognized some of the other authors, excited looks on their faces, appearing younger than I remembered. That made sense, naturally, because they were younger when they made their first sales. Out of curiosity, I pulled out Ian's picture; his maniacal grin was unmistakable.

Finally, I reached my picture. There I was, jumping into the air, with the telephone in my hand and a big smile on my face. The perfect souvenir of my first sale; after all, I couldn't have the check and cash it, too.

"I want the photograph," I said.

Stan stopped his lecture and pulled the picture out of my hands. Frowning, he said, "I can't give it to you, Michael. I keep them for myself. It reminds me of why I went into editing in the first place."

"Just this one, Stan? You won't miss it, and it means a lot to me." It did, too; my fiancée wasn't around when I heard the news, and this would be the best way to share the moment with her.

"Well..." Stan said, "you'll have to give me something in return."

"I don't have much money. I'm only a writer."

Stan laughed. "Oh, I wasn't thinking of money! Actually, all I'd want in return is another story from you. We've got a hole in the magazine for next month, and I need to fill it with something. The picture could be your payment."

My ears perked up. In exchange for the picture, Stan was going to publish *another* story of mine? "Sure! What kind of story would you like?"

"Could you give me a 'Probability Zero'? It's only a small hole, and anyway, you can make one of those short enough to be the right price."

I was confused. "What do you mean? The right price? What do you consider to be the right price for the photograph?"

"Oh," he said, with his ubiquitous smile and twinkle in his eyes, "I figure the picture is worth... about a thousand words."

I hit him with a Hugo rocket on my way out. It felt good.

Author's Note

This story should serve as its own Author's Note, but here's a little more about it.

It was my second appearance in *Analog*. To Stanley Schmidt's knowledge, this was the only time a writer's second appearance in the magazine was about their first appearance in the magazine. I think I managed the sale because after he read the story, Stan counted the words and decided it was close enough.

The story brings back a lot of memories; Ian and Scott were the assistant editors at *Analog* at the time, and Sydney was a Clarion classmate who has since passed away, alas.

As I read it today, I find it a bit juvenile but also humorous. I hope it made you laugh.

Publisher's Note

As the publisher, I had absolutely no say in what stories were accepted for this book (I left that to Tom and Judith as the editors). I didn't know this story was going to be included until I found myself counter-signing Michael's contract and writing him a check. And then it brought back memories.

Publishing in general, and science fiction publishing in particular, are often viewed as incestuous industries. In the case of this story, a lot of that comes through quite clearly. At the time Michael wrote the story, I was the Associate Editor of Analog, and had been working there for five years. Editor Stanley Schmidt had been at the helm of the magazine for sixteen years. I had made my first sale to Analog as a writer three years earlier.

I left Analog about the time this story was published, to start up my own magazine, Artemis. But as I was telling Stan I had to go (there was no room to be promoted, because the editorial staff was so small), he asked "Can I send you a story?" That story, "Generation Gap," appeared in the first issue of Artemis (and earned Stan his second Nebula and first Hugo Award nominations for writing). During Artemis's three-year run, Michael never managed to sell me a story, so this is the first time I'm publishing one of his works.

So we've entangled our various writing, editing, and publishing careers—Stan, Michael, and I—and it's thrilling to have both this story and Stan's "Throw Me a Bone" in this book. Now we just have to put Michael in an editorial position to publish stories by Stan and by me.

—Ian Randal Strock

A Right Jolly Old…

James L. Cambias

I stopped in my favorite coffee shop the day after Christmas, trying to get a little work done, but unfortunately I ran into Cecil. Cecil's not precisely a friend; he hangs out in the same coffee shops I hang out in, and we've had a few conversations. But I don't seek him out.

This time, however, he positively bounced over to where I was unpacking my laptop and grabbed the seat on the other side of the table. "How was Christmas?"

"Oh, fine," I said. "And yours?"

He looked at me very steadily, and said "I had the best Christmas I have ever had in my life."

"That's nice," I said. "Family come to visit?"

"No. I spent Christmas Eve alone, in fact. Put up my stocking kind of as a joke to myself. But I got the best Christmas present ever." He took a breath before continuing. "Do you ever wonder about where the idea of Santa Claus comes from?" he asked.

"Coke?"

"No! They're just jumping on the bandwagon. No, it all goes back to the poem."

"'The Night Before Christmas.'"

"'A Visit from St. Nicholas,' actually.[1] By Clement Moore. Written in 1823. That's important. But it's weird, if you think about it. Moore wasn't some Hallmark hack—he was a scholar of ancient languages, politically connected, owned half of Manhattan, taught at a theological seminary. Why did he suddenly crank out a catchy verse about Santa Claus? And why leave out anything connected to the actual saint?"

"I dunno," I said.

---

1. If you really want to get pedantic, it should be "An Account of a Visit from St. Nicholas." Or you can just call it "The Night Before Christmas" like normal people.

"Remember the year, 1823. That's the same year Caspar David Friedrich paints *The Polar Sea*."

"I don't see the connection," I said. People say that to Cecil a lot.

"Polar expeditions! Santa Claus! Do I have to draw a picture? The Royal Navy sent three separate expeditions to the Arctic in 1818. And that same year in Ohio, John Symmes sits down and writes to Congress urging them to fund an American polar expedition to look for the hole at the Pole leading into the hollow Earth."

"You think the Royal Navy was looking for Santa Claus in the Hollow Earth?"[2]

"You're closer than you think. Remember, Moore hadn't written his poem yet when those expeditions went north. Assuming he *really* wrote it.[3] But in 1811, right *before* the Royal Navy got so interested in the Arctic, there's a novel about a polar explorer whose ship is caught in the ice, who hears a fantastic story from a man he encounters crossing the ice cap in pursuit of a monstrous figure."

A memory from high school English class rose dimly in my head. "Wait, that's—"

"*Frankenstein*.[4] Very good. I don't know where Mary Shelley got her information, but she and her husband were connected to pretty much all of Europe's intellectual and political elite. It could have been Joseph Grimm, or maybe Prime Minister Perceval let something slip before he was assassinated.[5]"

"So Frankenstein—" I began.

"No, the *Monster*. Adam, the being Frankenstein created. Finds Symmes's Hole at the Pole.[6]"

---

2. They were looking for the Northwest Passage to the Pacific Ocean, because somebody finally looked at the terrain in Central America and realized how hard it would be to dig a canal with nothing but pickaxes and shovels.

3. Yes, he really wrote it.

4. Or, *The Modern Prometheus*. I can use Wikipedia, too.

5. His assassin had spent time in the Arctic... no. That just leads to Crazytown.

6. Cecil stole this one lock, stock, and barrel from Howard Waldrop.

I didn't want to go down that particular rabbit hole. Stick to the original question. "How does that connect with your best Christmas present ever?"

Cecil ticked items off on his fingers. "Here's the timeline: Frankenstein—whoever he really was—builds his creature about 1771. Murders ensue. They chase each other off into the Arctic some time before Mary writes the novel. I'm guessing her viewpoint guy Captain Walton is a stand-in for Commander Skeffington Lutwidge, who made an Arctic voyage in 1773. Lewis Carroll's uncle, by the way."

Down the rabbit hole, I thought, and then forced myself not to think about it.

"Frankenstein dies on the ice, Adam steals his body and pushes on. He finds Symmes's Hole, and makes contact with the Lemurians inside. Just a few years later, Clement Moore writes about a mysterious fur-cloaked figure distributing gifts. Obviously Adam has gotten ahold of Lemurian super-science, or maybe the lost civilization of Thule, or Deros. Deros are kind of like elves. It doesn't matter. There's always some lost civilization where you need one.[7] But the Lemurians have a reputation for doing astral projection, and you'd need that. The reindeer are obviously a cover story."

"Cover for what?"

He looked at me like I was retarded. "Flying saucers, of course. Duh."

I hurried to drop that particular subject. "I don't get it. Why would Frankenstein's Monster be putting presents in people's stockings?"

"Read the book! The Monster isn't evil, he's *naive.* Sometimes he tries to do good, he's just kind of inept about it. After killing his creator and finding a new world, he must have had some kind of moral awakening. He wants to make amends, so he starts giving presents. Just like a little kid, only with superhuman strength and intelligence, equipped with Lemurian vril[8]-science and an army of Deros. Along the way he puts on a little weight and grows a beard."

"Okay, Cecil. It's a fun theory. Santa Claus is really Frankenstein's creation living inside Symmes's Hole at the Pole and using lost

---

7. So very true.

8. First introduced in a novel by Edward Bulwer-Lytton, of "It was a dark and stormy night" fame.

civilization technology to zoom around the world in a flying saucer giving out presents. You should put it on your blog."

His face lit up at that. "I *did!* I put it up back at the beginning of the month! And that's what makes *this* the best Christmas present *ever!"* He dug in his pocket and held it up for me to see. "I found it in my stocking yesterday morning!"

It was a lump of coal.

Author's Note

This story began life as a Christmas card mailed to friends and relations in 2013. One of those friends-and-relations was Steve Popkes, who recommended it to editor Tom Easton for his anthology *Conspiracy!* (NESFA Press, 2016). I heard about it when Dr. Easton informed me he wanted to buy it. Easiest sale I ever made. Cecil Street is also the main character in my short story "Parsifal (Prix Fixe)" which appeared in *The Magazine of Fantasy & Science Fiction* in 2006.

Space Opera

Daniel M. Kimmel

The meteor heading toward Earth spelled certain doom. Its massive size and velocity was such that its impact would end all life on the planet, if not actually tear the very Earth apart. Located outside Pluto's orbit, the meteor was headed for an inevitable date with disaster for humanity. Our only hope was to blast it to pieces long before it worked its way through the solar system. Our ship, the *Götterdämmerung*, was equipped with a series of four plasma torpedoes that had to be fired according to precise calculations. We needed not only to shatter the meteor, but also to do it in such a way that the debris dispersed across the Solar System instead of continuing on course to Earth. If we did this right, we would create an outer asteroid belt. If we miscalculated in any way, we would set a bombardment of meteor pieces hurtling toward the Earth that the planet might survive, but humanity would not.

I had signed aboard the ship knowing that this was a mission from which we might not return. We were a crew who knew what was at stake and knew what we had to do. If we failed, it would be more than a disaster. The final curtain would have fallen on Earth without hope of a revival or an encore.

We were moments away from our rendezvous with destiny when our fearless captain, Giacomo Puccini, rose from his seat on the command deck and turned to address the entire crew. All comm systems were given over to his dramatic message.

"*Ci stiamo avvicinando la meteora…*," he sang in his beautiful tenor. I had no idea what he was saying, as my knowledge of Italian was limited to *arrivederci* and *veal scallopini*.

"Subtitles, please," I ordered the monitor, which began real time translation of his aria. This was his final call to the crew to do our utmost to save not only our families back on Earth, but the rich legacy of humanity which La Scala, the planetary space authority, had put so much effort into trying to preserve.

"We are approaching the meteor…" the subtitles read.

The lighting on the captain subtly changed as he sang, "*È il momento di eseguire la missione per la quale siamo stati addestrati…*"

"It is time to perform the mission for which we were trained…," appeared at the bottom of the screen. I wish he had simply transmitted the libretto to the crew, as it would have saved time, but this was the captain's big moment.

Suddenly a chorus appeared behind him. It was only a dozen or so men and women, but they were representing the entire crew. For some reason, they were singing in French.

"*Nous sommes prêts à donner notre vie pour la Terre et l'honneur de notre glorieux capitaine,*" they sang.

It took a moment for the ship's computer to adjust to the change of language. A moment later, the translation appeared: "We are prepared to lay down our lives for Earth and the honor of our glorious captain."

Incongruously, he sang his reply in Italian. "*Sono orgoglioso di voi, il mio equipaggio. Sono onorata di guidarvi in battaglia.*" ("You do me proud. I am honored to lead you into battle.")

This was all very inspiring, but my big moment was coming up, and I couldn't afford to miss my cue. The fate of mankind hung in the balance.

"*Sono i siluri al plasma pronto per essere licenziato?*" ("Are the plasma torpedoes ready to be fired?")

A mezzosoprano whom I only knew as Torpedo 1 responded, "*Bereit auf Ihren Befehl, mein Kapitän.*"

A bass listed on the roster as Torpedo 2 similarly replied, "Ready on your command, my captain."

Torpedo 3 struck an atonal note in Japanese, "*Watashi no kyaputen, anata no meirei de junbi ga dekimashita.*"

Finally it was my big moment, for which I had been rehearsing for months. As the fill light bathed me in a greenish glow, I faced the communicator and sang my readiness to do my duty, "*Pronto il vostro comando, mio capitano.*"

"*Sul mio ordine,*" responded the captain. ("On my order.") This led to a beautiful round as we four torpedo operators repeated our readiness to serve in each of our languages. Suddenly the lights dimmed throughout the ship—except for the spotlight on the captain—as he movingly sang, "*Fuoco. Fuoco. Fuoco.*"

I did not need to read the subtitles to know we had been given the command to fire. We each pressed the appropriate buttons as the entire crew began praying in Italian, *"Preghiamo che il nostro obiettivo è vero. La Terra deve vivere. Preghiamo che il nostro obiettivo è vero. La Terra deve vivere."* As I sang I felt the words deep inside me: We pray that our aim be true. Let the Earth live.

After the missiles were fired, the ship took off at near light speed toward Earth, trying to get as far away from the impending explosions as possible. Even so, the ship was severely shaken. Singing was impossible, even if the discordant music had permitted vocal accompaniment.

At last the ship righted course. The computer readouts indicated our mission had been a success. The meteor had been destroyed. Earth had been spared. Alas, this happy result was not without tragedy. Captain Puccini, at the moment of his greatest triumph, had been attacked by Science Officer Verdi, who was jealous of the captain's relationship with Lt. Mimi, our communications officer. During the destruction of the meteor, Verdi had stabbed Puccini, who killed his attacker but was himself fatally wounded.

On our screens, Captain Puccini made his dramatic exit, *"Siamo riusciti anche se devo pagare il prezzo per il mio amore. Ti saluto, il mio equipaggio valente."*

I had to look at the subtitles. I knew my own line in Italian, but I had learned it phonetically. "We have succeeded even as I must pay the price for my love. I salute you, my valiant crew." The captain embraced his beloved Mimi as the spotlight dimmed and he expired.

It was a most dramatic mission, but I think it will be my last. When we return to Earth I'm going to put in a transfer to the *Fledermaus*. I think I'm much more cut out for space operetta.

Author's Note

Film critic Daniel M. Kimmel is the author of seven books, including the Hugo finalist *Jar Jar Binks Must Die... and Other Observations about Science Fiction Movies*, and *Shh! It's a Secret: a Novel about Aliens, Hollywood, and the Bartender's Guide*, which was a finalist for the Compton Crook Award. His latest is *Time on My Hands: My Misadventures in Time Travel*.

Musicians End the World

Gerald Warfield

I'd been on the L.A. Police Force six months to the day when our monitor picked up residue from a concussion wave. Back then, c-waves were fired from shoulder amp cannons, and the blast signatures lit up monitors for a hundred kilometers, so we were on them pretty quick.

"Hold on, Marge." My partner, Stu, reached back for the Flypack. "You got the last one."

I could fly circles around him, but he was right. I shrugged, and he jumped out, leaving me to bring the scooter. First report came in before I was halfway there: hysterical woman crying her son had gone hissy and was shooting up the neighborhood.

"Got a visual," Stu cut in. "Musta dropped his cannon. He's retreating to…" The coordinates followed.

I was impressed he'd gotten there so fast. I was less impressed a minute later when I found his body. The CL took me straight to him: face up on a flight pad, his chest caved in.

"God damn it!" I flipped the e-call, leapt off the scooter, and snatched up the med kit. Ripping it open, I pulled out the freezer shroud. My hands shook as I raised his head and slipped the shroud over him; never used one of those things except in simulations. His face looked fine, like he was sleeping. I snapped the safety, and it frosted over instantly. "Don't go. Stay with me, Stu," I said, gripping his shoulder. Best scenario, six months regrowing his vitals. Worst, my fiancé Mario lost a brother and, incidentally, best man at our wedding.

"He didn't mean to!" A woman peeked from behind an elevated bed of nasturtiums. Her over-sized head and spindly limbs indicated a mental.

I scooted close and released the shield on her side so we could talk. "What's the make on the cannon?" I could calibrate my shield for it.

"He hasn't got anything," she said. "He was just rehearsing."

Yeah, right. "He didn't punch out my partner without a fucking cannon. What's he got?"

"I don't know." She wrung her hands. "He's just a musician. I think he took a little too much star dust...."

The prodigy's life story was interrupted by a blast that rocked my shield so hard it bowled me over sideways. Good thing I had moved closer to mommy, or she'd have been splattered all over the wall. As it was, she was just splattered with nasturtiums.

But she was right; he didn't have a cannon. The kid high-tailed it back into what looked like a hanger.

"What's your situation," snapped my com.

"Stu's down, in a freeze lock. Send a pod fast. Concussion caved in his chest. Got a berserker. Don't see a cannon. I'm shielding his mother."

"Can you contain him 'til we get there?"

"I think so. I'll try to gas him."

About then, the guy bursts out the door screaming. Tall, ragged-looking with stringy black hair, he didn't have a cannon, but I knuckled down by instinct. The impact didn't knock me over this time. He was still coming, but when he spotted Stu he let out a shriek and gestured with one hand, his fingers wide. Stu's body scudded across the launchpad, spinning. Please God, he didn't hit him in the head.

I wouldn't have believed it if I hadn't seen it with my own eyes. No cannon. He just gestured like he was some kinda wizard or something.

While he was distracted with Stu, I got off a gas pellet. When the thing popped, the kid looked up, all wild like, and raised a hand. I knew I was in for it. Stupid, because I had my shield up, but I was right to worry. The shock knocked me clean back on my ass.

The gas got him at that point, and he fell forward onto the concrete.

"Ludwig!" Mommy rushed out from the nasturtiums and scooped up the bugger, who was bleeding from his nose. I didn't bother to warn her, and then she reeled and crashed on top of him. Probably enjoyed the gas.

I scrambled over to Stu. His head had imploded in the freeze bag. He wouldn't be regrowing any vitals—and he wouldn't be Mario's best man. "Damn, damn," I cursed, and shook my head in disbelief.

Security would have censored what happened next, but a fly cam got to the scene about the time I did. The first incontrovertible evidence of concussive wave generation was right there for everybody to see. The cam also caught me kicking Ludwig in the ribs. That's what got me bumped off the force. Funny thing, I coulda saved the world right then—if I'd have just killed the bastard.

My perp was the first to make the leap directly from nerve impulses to concussion waves—all it took was a bass amp converter, no cannon necessary. "All you're doing is amplifying your own song," he's supposed to have said at his trial. Eventually, he taught his fellow inmates, who turned out to be better at it than he was. San Quentin didn't survive their first jam session.

My little cabin in the woods is still standing, partly because it's wedged deep in a gorge. Bad for when it rains, but good for when the c-waves come bouncing over the hills. All the trees up on the ridge have been flattened.

That cabin was to have been our survivalist retreat, but Mario got caught three months ago when the band from Northridge flattened Pasadena. He was never reported dead. They don't check bodies for ID any more.

I remember reading about when they invented old-fashioned guns and gunpowder. People thought a weapon that powerful—when anybody could shoot anybody else—would be the end of the world. Well, when people can just think a weapon of mass destruction, it's only a matter of time. Whenever the muses settle down out there, I wonder if there'll be anything left at all.

Author's Note

Composer and writer Gerald Warfield's short stories have appeared in many online venues and print anthologies including *NewMyths*, *Bewildering Stories*, *Every Day Fiction*, and *Metaphorosis*. "The Poly Islands" won second prize in the first quarter of the 2011 Writers of the Future contest. The same year, his humorous story "The Origin of Third Person in Paleolithic Epic Poetry" took first place in the Grammar Girl short story contest. Gerald published music textbooks and how-to books in investing before turning to fiction. He is a graduate of the Odyssey Writers Workshop (2010), Taos Toolbox, and a member of SFWA.

Nif's World

Lawrence Watt-Evans

Nif watched, enraptured, as the colors poured out through the worldstalk, blue and green and white. Her fingers tightened around her companions' hands in a final squeeze before they separated into their individual environment bubbles and soared apart, each bound for her own sprouting worldlet.

Nif did not take the first worldlet she saw, nor the second; she knew what she wanted, and in time she spotted it. Ahead, a little to one side, a worldlet was blooming outward, already a full sphere and approaching its final dimensions, with all the green-coated land on one side, the shining blue of the ocean on the other. That was what she needed, a world with only a single continent.

She flapped a wing and steered for it. Her wings were non-functional in the vacuum of space, of course, but the environment bubble registered the motion and fed the information to her propulsion unit.

She exulted at the sight of her chosen miniplanet. She had been planning this for pentads, dreaming and scheming for the day when she would at last sail into the pocket universe, the shaping power placed ready in her mind. She knew that her teachers doubted her talents, and she was determined to prove what she could do.

The purple mists of ylem were clearing as she swooped down toward the globe she had selected and prepared to nip it free of its nurturing tendrils.

Once she cut it free of the stalk there was no going back; that would commit her to shape this worldlet and no other. She did not hesitate, but sheared the stalk quickly and let the planet spin free.

It was all hers. She was on her own now. In her classroom assignments she had never been alone, not really; she had had her textmemories to refer to, and more importantly, she had had Qui and Skir to help out.

Now, though, her two best friends were off to their own worldlets, and she had nothing she could draw on but her own skills and talent and desire.

The desire was there, certainly. She wanted to be an artist, a world-shaper, more than anything else she could imagine. She had always wanted that. The talent, she was certain, was inside her somewhere, lurking within, buried still beneath the awkwardness of her youth, awaiting an opportunity to blossom forth.

The skills, however, were lacking. She knew that. She simply was not very proficient with the shaping power. Her conceptions were not clear enough, not detailed enough, for the enabling mechanisms to follow them through quickly and easily. She had to go over every little thought and image, over and over, correcting flaws, filling in gaps, and even reshaping concepts. Often, unfortunately, her concepts didn't work.

It was an unfathomable wonder to her that Qui could bring forth her ornate creations in a single sweeping work, whole invented realities purring and ticking like fine machinery—though of course, until now, Qui had never had to fill an entire *world*. In her earlier projects, though, Qui had never been troubled by details, and Nif had no doubt that world-shaping would go as well for her. Qui's creations always worked, and worked right the first time, without tinkering.

Skir was almost as good, creating her works not all at once, as Qui did, but in a smooth progression, like a flower opening.

Nif's were more like a child's card-houses, rickety and uneven and likely to collapse under close inspection.

All the same, skills lacking or not, she had made it this far. She had reached the Competition. She had skirted the very edges of cheating to do it, of course, getting the most help that she could possibly be allowed from Qui and Skir and the household AIs. She had spent pentads plotting and planning, thinking what she could do that would impress the judges with her undeveloped raw talent, that would show she had the audacity to be a fine world-shaper even if she lacked the polish of her competitors.

She had known that any wholly original concept would not work. Under the intense pressure of the Competition, with the terrifyingly short time limit, she knew that she could only botch one of her own muddled ideas. She wouldn't have the time to go back and patch it together after the initial shaping.

She had searched for something she could adapt, instead, a concept she could take, ready-made, to shape a world. She had dug back through history and myth for something clear and simple, so that she could handle it, but so stunningly appropriate and powerful that the judges would have no choice but to recognize its value.

And, at last, she had found what she wanted.

She approached her chosen worldlet and studied it.

Yes, it was just as it should be. Ready to drop from the stalk, it was roughly three kilometers in diameter—in the warped reality of the Competition's artificially-opened pocket universe, that would support a fully-realized, miniature, Earthlike environment.

It had a molten metal core, a thick stone mantle, a fragile crust of tectonically-active plates that she could manipulate if she chose, and enough water to cover almost four-fifths of the surface with oceans, all in perfect miniature. The land surfaces, both dry and suboceanic, were coated with a thin layer of easily-modified, high-speed genetic material, ready for her to shape.

She reached out, in communion with the shaping power, and began to bring forth her dream. The gene-stuff grew and blossomed at her command, burgeoning wildly, until it had entirely covered her world's single continent with a tame, peaceful, luxuriant garden. She needed no deserts, no mountains, no badlands for her creation, simply a single continent-sized garden.

When that was done she reached out again—thinking, as she did, that Qui was probably done already, with some magnificent, intricate work—and raised up fauna from the newly-formed, still-unstable flora. Beasts that crawled and walked and flew, that swam or burrowed, she brought forth as many as she could devise, all herbivorous, all calm, placid, peaceful. Her world was to be a paradise, not a battlefield.

When the beasts were finished, adequately if not well, she concentrated on the small open plain at the center of the single continent. There she put a single great tree, a tree bearing biocybernetic fruit. Each fruit carried a semi-sentient pseudo-organism, self-contained, which, if ingested by a humanoid, would become a symbiote bonded to the human nervous system, feeding information and the accumulated moral knowledge of the human race into the eater's mind.

She had worked on that aspect, all by itself, for more than a pentad, in planning her project. She had mentioned something to Qui about her preparations, and Qui had laughed.

"You can't plan everything, Nif," she had said. "You need to see what fits on the world you choose. The judges want to see us make the best use of the material we're given, not just impose our own order upon it."

That was all very well for Qui, Nif thought, but not everyone was as skillful as she.

She was ready for the centerpiece of her work now. She reached out to a pair of near-apes, one male and one female, that she had kept handy, and placed them beneath her biocybernetic tree. There she reshaped them, shifting and sorting their genes until they were virtually indistinguishable from true humans, save for their size, the speed at which they lived, and the peculiar nature of the other-universal matter that made up their bodies.

She herself, of course, was not exactly a true human, since her ancestors had been modifying their genes to suit their whims, or the whims of fashion, for millennia. Her wings were the most obvious manifestation of that. She was not interested in creating beings in her own image, however, and stuck closely to the natural genetic blueprint for humanity, as it had originally evolved.

Adam and Eve, she called them when she was done, and the worldlet, of course, was Eden. She registered this name with the Competition's administrators mere moments before the three judges sailed into view, their environment bubbles gleaming golden in the warm light of the artificial sun.

Nif saw them approaching and waited expectantly. As she had been instructed she ascended, watching but well away from her work, so as to allow the judges their first look without interference. When they were ready she would swoop down and explain it all, tell them of the ancient myths, explain how her Tree of the Knowledge of Good and Evil worked, and then, modestly, she would await their assessment.

She was certain that she had created her masterpiece. Qui would probably outdo her, and Zik, and maybe Skir, but there were a dozen openings to be had this time around, and she would surely rate one of them.

The judges were taking their first good look at her world, and she found herself unable to resist. She had a trace of the shaping power left, and she used it, almost without meaning to, to tap into their private communications as they judged her Eden.

The first judge spoke almost immediately after reaching the planet, before she could possibly have seen more than the most obvious features, and her words froze Nif's heart.

"Oh, Creation!" she said. "Not Adam and Eve again!"

"That's the third Garden of Eden this time around," the second judge remarked, bemused.

"You'd think the kids would learn," the third said, "but every time it's the same old things, Eden or dinosaurs. Don't they realize we've seen that a hundred times before?" He registered a rejection for Nif's world; neither of his fellows countered it. Without speaking to Nif at all, they prepared to move on to the next worldlet.

Author's Note

Lawrence Watt-Evans is the author of fifty novels and over a hundred short stories, including fantasy, SF, horror, and more. He is probably best known for the Legends of Ethshar series, and won the short story Hugo in 1988 for "Why I Left Harry's All-Night Hamburgers." He's a full-time writer based in Maryland.

"Nif's World" was the result of a challenge at a long-ago SF convention to come up with a story based on a specific painting in the art show.

RELIGION

People spend an astonishing amount of time thinking and arguing about religion. So do science fiction writers, as they wonder: What is right? What would Jesus do? Can religion be a metaphor for the artist's life?

Kayonga's Decision

Dave Creek

Why does that mass of stars seem to be reaching out to me? Kayonga Tedesco wondered as he floated within the clear viewing bubble of the starcraft *Belyanka*. With the lights out and giant Jupiter on the opposite side of the ship, the full glory of the stars shone before him, and one particularly large grouping of those points of fire appeared to him as misshapen arms advancing toward him. *My own personal constellation*, he thought.

Kayonga knew this was an illusion borne of a restless mind searching for patterns as he waited for the priest to arrive. All the same, he accepted the image as a comfort, something he'd found in short supply in recent days.

The viewing bubble's door slid aside and the priest floated in, pushing off against the edge of the doorway with a practiced ease. He landed next to Kayonga and offered his hand to shake. "Father Dominic Clarkson."

"Kayonga Tedesco."

Father Dominic indicated the starfield beyond the clear walls. "Beautiful, isn't it?"

Kayonga decided not to share his impression of the stars reaching out for him. "Almost beyond Human understanding, I'd say."

"I believe it takes us back to our most primitive days. When all the stars were *above* us, not all around."

"Uh… how do I go about this?"

"Typically, a Catholic says, 'Forgive me, Father, for I have sinned.' And you tell me how long it's been since your last confession."

"I'm not Catholic."

"Oh. Well, as ship's chaplain, I can do any number of flavors."

"I've described myself as a sect of one. And we were just looking at its scripture."

"I think I understand," Father Dominic said. "Then let me just ask how I can help you."

"I'm scheduled to leave on this ship, to become an explorer. But I'm uncertain as to whether I should."

"What's caused that uncertainty?"

"Haven't you heard of my actions, Father? Don't you know why I come to you so ashamed?"

"Never mind what I've heard. I want to hear your story as you need to tell it."

"Very well, Father."

It involved a rescue attempt gone awry deep in Jupiter's atmosphere (Kayonga told Father Dominic), and it threatened to become a double disaster. And I found myself the only person in a position to bring help in time.

It meant running to the only shuttle on Callisto Base that could get fired up and ready to go in time, and even then bypassing a dozen safety protocols and pre-flight procedures. Not to mention leaving without a co-pilot, which was strictly against protocol. But I had to lift as quickly as possible from that moon's dark, pock-marked surface.

Once I had the gravitic drive straining to erase the distance between Callisto and Jupiter, I got on the comm to my friend Michael Shannon, and found myself fighting to keep my voice steady and professional, not letting the fear I felt for him leak through: "What's your shuttle's status?"

Michael's response came back through a background of static: "Drive's out. We're sinking slowly so far, but sinking all the same. We've got no chance of making it on our own."

Michael and his co-pilot, Donna Gage, had launched earlier on a mission to help five Jupiter whales, three of them seriously injured.

Humans from Callisto Base had been communicating with the whales for several years, and Michael and Donna responded immediately to their call for help, only to find themselves traveling through a series of thunderheads nearly fifty kilometers tall that was generating lightning far stronger than any storms on Earth.

They took the risk.

And a bolt ten times as hot as the surface of the sun struck their shuttle, knocking out most of its systems. The craft immediately began to sink into the depths of Jupiter's atmosphere. Soon the pressure there would crush the shuttle. It was slim consolation that it would only take a fraction of a second, too short a time for the Human nervous system to perceive it or feel any pain.

"What about the whales?" I asked as Jupiter loomed ahead, with some of its yellow, red, and brown bands of clouds as wide as six hundred kilometers. I was guiding the craft to an area of the giant planet several hundred kilometers north of the Great Red Spot, which was a storm as wide as Earth itself.

Michael said, "They're having a tough time of it. Two of them trying to lift three others—they're all getting pretty tired."

Adult Jupiter whales could grow to be half a kilometer long. Their bodies were filled with helium and heavier gases, allowing them to glide within the depths of the gas giant's atmosphere.

Three of them had flown down into calmer skies where they fed on much smaller lifeforms. One of them, however, a youngster, strayed from the calm and wandered into an area where winds topped out at just over 360 kilometers an hour. The young whale's body couldn't take the buffeting, and two of the adults also ventured into the high wind area to rescue him. They were injured, in turn, and two more adults also risked their lives extracting all three of the stricken whales.

Now the two uninjured Jupiter whales were trying to bring the three injured ones up to calmer climes. They'd hoped Michael's shuttle could use its enticement beams to help lift them, but now that craft needed rescue, as well.

"How much time do you have left?" I asked.

Michael's voice was unsteady as he said, "About eight minutes until enough systems break down that we're crushed."

I measured his speed against the distance I had to cover. "I can just make it."

Another voice came over the datalink: "This is the Human Kayonga Tedesco?"

One of the Jupiter whales, I realized. "Yes, it is."

"This is Entai, the mother of my pod. We are all weakening. We will fall into the world before your shuttle does. I fear all of us will die."

Another quick check of speed and distance, and I said, "I can't bring you up and the Human craft as well."

"I am looking out for my pod. I will sacrifice myself if you can save the other four of us, then the Humans."

I shook my head. "I still wouldn't be able to save both them and the Human shuttle. Michael, are you *sure* of that timeline?"

"Just seven minutes now," Michael said. "Are you headed this way?"

A chill went through my body. "I... gotta decide!"

"*Decide*? C'mon, man, your mom's like an extra parent to me. What would she say?"

I realized exactly what she would say, as memories welled up:

My mother letting me decide, at age seven, whether to "tell" on another boy who'd stolen a ring from one of her friends. I told, even though I knew some of my friends would shun me.

Age fourteen, taking on a 17-year-old who'd knocked a young boy to the ground. I took a pounding, but the 17-year-old left the younger boy alone after that.

Michael's voice was back in my ear: "Kayonga, we're friends! Donna's got sisters, nieces back home! You can't be considering—"

"That's a whole family of whales—there's... there's..."

"Just two of us? I don't like putting it like this, but—Donna and I, we're, you know."

Human, I thought.

Entai's voice broke in again. "As someone who is a different species from you, I understand if you save the Humans. But as a mother, I ask you to save my youngest, Itrak, and my other children Lilyn, Therach, and Serild."

I made my decision. I set the shuttle on a new course. "Michael—Donna—I'm sorry."

"Goddam it, Kayonga! How can you do this? I—I loved you!"

As I neared the Jupiter whales and activated the shuttle's enticement beam, all I could say was, "You had it right. About what my mother would say."

I remembered my mother praising me, hugging me after I revealed the identity of the thieving child, remembered her telling me how proud of me she was as she treated my cuts and bruises from the bully's beating.

And as Kayonga's shuttle approached the whales and its enticement beam drew them upwards toward safety, as I wished I could press my hands against my ears to shut out Michael's final, screaming protests, I remembered just what she told me each time: "You can usually tell the right choice to make," she said. "It's the one that hurts the most."

* * *

As he finished his story, Kayonga floated with his eyes tightly closed against the brilliance of the stars. Father Dominic said, "Do you really believe that?"

Kayonga looked at the priest. "I don't know what to believe, Father. In the last few days I've been called a murderer. A traitor to my own race. Why would God test me in such a way?"

"The eternal question. All religions must try to answer it at some point. I'm partial to one of the Psalms: 'Your word is a lamp to my feet and a light to my path.'"

Kayonga rubbed his eyes. "That doesn't seem to provide an answer, Father. Just comfort. And I'm not a Christian."

"All right, then. Other flavors. The Quran says, 'No calamity befalls on the earth or in yourselves but is inscribed in the Book of Decrees before we bring it into existence.'"

"So the pen writes, and we're helpless before it? That's not even a comfort."

"All right. The Buddha taught that we suffer because we desire something."

"Is desiring not to be thought of as a murderer so wrong?"

"I'm running out of flavors, Kayonga. One of my dearest friends is an atheist. Sometimes I think he sums it up perfectly."

"How's that?"

"Shit happens."

Kayonga smiled. "If only it were that simple. Maybe I should take heart from an explorer from several decades ago. Alexander Barron—you know the name?"

"Of course. Made his name out here in Jupiter space. Flew the first missions into its atmosphere."

"He once said, 'I've never believed in God; but I believe in Creation.'" Kayonga aimed his gaze toward the stars again. "I believe I understand what he meant. The very idea of God mystifies me now."

Father Dominic said, "But you see His works before you."

"And that guides my decision," Kayonga said. "I'll become an explorer. I'll head out among the stars." He pressed his hand against the surface of the bubble, as if he could touch that mass of light that appeared to be reaching toward him. "They, at least, are willing to reveal themselves to me."

Author's Note

Dave Creek is the author of the novels *Some Distant Shore*, *Chanda's Awakening*, and *The Unmoving Stars*, along with the short story collections *A Glimpse of Splendor* and *The Human Equations*.

He's also published a series of novellas, including *The Silent Sentinels*, *A Crowd of Stars* (2016 Imadjinn Award winner), *The Fallen Sun*, and *Tranquility*.

His short stories have appeared in *Analog Science Fiction and Fact* and *Apex* magazines, and the anthologies *Far Orbit Apogee*, *Touching the Face of the Cosmos*, and *Dystopian Express*.

Find out more about Dave's work at www.davecreek.com, on Facebook, and on Twitter, @DaveCreek.

In the "real world," Dave is a retired television news producer.

Dave lives in Louisville with his wife Dana, son Andy, and two sleepy cats—Hedwig and Hemingway.

Ten Things I Know About Jesus

Steven Popkes

#1: *Jesus doesn't have a lot of parties.*

We don't have a lot of friends over. Every now and then I bring home someone from school. Jesus is always very nice and makes cookies. Jesus makes tremendous cookies. Nothing beats them. Except maybe his cakes. He doesn't like crowds of people.

Even so, every few weeks is poker night. Then, his three friends come over: Satan, Lazarus, and Albert. They play poker in the den. Jesus normally doesn't allow smoking in the house, but Satan smokes like a chimney. Jesus insists that Satan confine the smoke to the den, which he does reluctantly. It gives the room a weird effect to stand just outside and see the wall of smoke stop in the doorway.

On poker night I serve the food and the beer. I can stay in and listen—Jesus doesn't mind. I think it makes Lazarus uncomfortable. I'm not sure. He's so quiet you can never tell. Albert ignores me. Albert's all about the cards. Usually, I bring a tray to the den door and hand it to Jesus through the smoke. The next morning the smoke is gone. You can't even smell it.

Satan plays to win. When he's having a good night, Satan laughs at the rest of them. He smiles wickedly at me and says, "We'll play for you next, boy. You're going in the pot!" Jesus chuckles in a way that I know he would never allow it.

Most nights, though, Satan doesn't win that much. As soon as he starts getting enough ahead that Jesus disapproves, the cards change on him and he'll lose back to just barely over the others. Satan's accused Jesus of cheating more than once, but I've seen Satan himself try all sorts of ways to cheat. They never work. He'll win for a while and then, out of the blue, Lazarus will hit a streak. Or Albert. Sometimes Jesus wins a few hands. Most nights he breaks even.

They play until very late—I'm usually asleep on the sofa when they file clumsily past, trying not to wake me. Satan always leaves first, peels rubber and is off down the street. Lazarus and Albert follow. Jesus cleans up.

I often pretend to be asleep so I can catch him in a miracle. I never do.

#2: Jesus lives in Higbee, Missouri.

I live there, too. It's a little five-room house. Higbee is a little town near Moberly. I have my room. Jesus has his. There's a kitchen, a living room, and a den. There's a barn where we keep the car. Jesus drives me to school every day.

We have about a hundred acres of farmland and forty acres of woodlot. Jesus rents out most of it for farming.

We have a garden. Every spring, Jesus plants a big square in nothing but sunflowers. In the fall we harvest the seeds and snack on them all through the winter.

In the spring, we cut a couple of trees down in the woodlot, too. Every fall we harvest the driest of those trees, from perhaps four or five years ago, to use in the woodstove over the winter.

We have music but no television or video games. We have a stereo, a piano, a banjo, and a guitar. I play the piano and guitar. Jesus plays the banjo.

I've seen television and played video games at the houses of friends. I wish we had an X-Box.

#3: Jesus was crucified.

Jesus says that myths often come up exactly the opposite of what actually happened. He's seen it before. Somebody will drown crossing a river and a hundred years later there's a folktale about a knight crossing a river to die mysteriously on the other side. A hundred years after that the knight will cross the river by walking on water in his search for the Holy Grail. Actual events mean nothing. The story is shaped to some other need and only a seed remains.

Here's what happened to him.

Jesus was nailed up on the cross—that part was true—but he didn't die quickly and come back in three days. His side wasn't speared or any of that. Jesus hung on that cross for two weeks, three weeks, a month, and didn't die. Finally, there was enough muttering about it that Pilate had him cut down and brought to him. A few days later, Jesus walked out still alive. He left Jerusalem and the savior business behind. A month hanging on iron nails was enough. It would have been easier to die.

#4: *Jesus saved me.*

I don't know who my parents were. Jesus says he found me in a dumpster, newborn and bloody. He took me to the hospital and they checked me over pretty good. He held me while they tested me. They wanted to take me away, he says, but he'd decided he liked the feel of me sitting in his lap. It had been a while since he'd held a baby.

He decided to adopt me. That's the way he says it, too. Like it was as simple as adopting a cat or taking in a stray dog. For him, I guess, it was. Papers were suddenly signed and records changed mysteriously until he walked out of the hospital with me.

I don't know if I'm the first baby Jesus ever adopted or the hundred and first. I don't think it matters.

Jesus is my guardian. It says so on my birth certificate.

#5: *Jesus doesn't perform miracles.*

Or, at least, not often.

He's been around for a couple of thousand years. There's not much need for him to change any water into wine or raise the dead.

Jesus said that what led up to the crucifixion was his first and last foray into wholesale politics. He thinks people are like mules. They are very receptive to conversation if you can get their attention. In the case of a mule, attention is usually by the application of a two-by-four. In the case of people, miracles serve the same purpose.

One time when I was small I lost the use of my right hand. Jesus took me to the hospital. I had abscesses in my brain. No one could figure out where they came from. There was a kid down the hall that had been admitted for the same thing. I got worse and there came a point where I just don't remember anything.

I woke up in the hospital bed. Jesus was sitting next to the bed reading. I felt okay, though my right hand didn't work right.

That will get better with time, Jesus said. He was pretty calm about it.

I asked about the kid down the hall. Jesus told me he had died.

I thought about it for a long time. Did Jesus save me with a miracle? If he did, why didn't he save the kid down the hall? Even though I was glad to be alive, I wished the kid wasn't dead. The more I thought about it, the more I thought that I didn't like the idea of Jesus saving one kid (me) and letting another kid die. He should save everybody.

Then I thought, what if it was just random? What if he didn't do anything? What if it was just chance that I got better and that nameless kid died? My abscesses were a little smaller than his, maybe. Or weaker. Or in different parts of the brain.

After a while, I figured it must be random because Jesus making a choice between us made me feel too sad.

I never asked him which it was.

#6: Jesus doesn't go to church.

I've been a couple of times. I don't like it. The pictures of Jesus don't look like him. What the preachers say Jesus said doesn't sound like him. I keep quiet about Jesus in church. He never told me to; I just thought it was a good idea.

I asked him about churches once. He said he'd lived too long to go to church. He said he had nothing to do with them. After all, they were invented long after he'd left that whole business behind him.

How did they all get started? I asked.

He said it was like a long game of whispers—telephone, people called it now. That what came out of the end of the telephone didn't bear much resemblance to what went in. He said after a while, the story got so strong it drowned out the facts. People *always* believed a good story, whether it had anything behind it or not.

What I didn't like about the church was the way they always showed Jesus hanging from the nails on the cross. In the Baptist or the Methodist church, he looked sleepy or stunned. Sometimes he looked peaceful. In the Catholic Church, though, he looked like he was screaming.

So, I said. The Crucifixion. What was it like?

Jesus shook his head. You don't want to know.

#7: Jesus doesn't tell stories.

Jesus doesn't talk about himself much. He will answer any question I ask him. He doesn't hide anything, but he won't talk about it himself unless I ask him first. He says that I can say whatever I want to—nobody will believe me. As it is, Jesus being pretty dark-skinned, people think he's descended from Mexicans. I'm in the habit of not correcting them.

One day I went over to my friend Beryl's house. Her father used to work on the river down near Saint Louis, and he told story after story until we were laughing so hard we were crying. Beryl had to run to the bathroom so she didn't pee her pants. As it was, I don't think she made it. She never let on.

I came home and asked Jesus how come he never told stories.

He shrugged. He said nobody likes the stories he has to tell.

#8: Jesus is the Son of God.

Here in Missouri you can't throw a cat so you won't hit a preacher and you can't hit a baseball that it doesn't land in the yard of a church. One time coming back from Kansas City I counted seventeen billboards advertising churches and nineteen billboards advertising XXX dancing. I asked Jesus how come dancers outnumbered churches. He said *Vox Populi*. That was in October. Around July there were more billboards advertising fireworks than the churches and dancers put together.

So you can't walk around here without Jesus and God coming out in the same breath. When I finally understood how churches worked— Jesus, God and the Holy Spirit all welded together—I was pretty confused. I had this image of a Siamese twin sort of creature with four legs, four arms, and two heads with a pigeon glued on the back. I drew it out in class one day and the teacher wanted me to talk to my parents all about it. That afternoon. Before dinner.

When I asked Jesus if he was the Son of God, he said yes. He said calling someone the "Son of God" was like labeling that painful red flickering stuff "fire". The words don't tell you much. Of course, he said, the title did get you the opportunity to be hung up on nails for a month so you could contemplate the nature of things.

What about God? I asked.

God's the black box where you put things you don't understand, he said.

What about you? I asked. You've been around forever. You were crucified. They named *churches* after you.

He shrugged. I know how to open the box.

#9: Jesus has friends.

I don't know that Satan is Jesus' best friend. They don't always get along so well. Satan comes around more often than anyone else. He always brings a six pack or two, a quart of whiskey and a cigar. Unless it's poker night, Jesus insists Satan smoke outside. Satan likes to sit in a rocking chair on the porch, smoke his cigar, and drink until he's too drunk to stand. I've heard tell in churches that Satan is a supernatural creature—an angel gone bad. I'm familiar with the "gone bad" part, as I've had to clean up after him when he's drunk too much. The angel part is pretty hard to see.

He's not like Jesus. Satan doesn't have any problem performing miracles. A goat walks by and he snaps his fingers and all of a sudden it's got five legs instead of four. Satan laughs until he chokes. There was a dead coyote up the road from the house just covered in flies. It caused Satan no end of delight to bring those flies all the way to the porch and have them spell out bad words on the walkway. After a while, the flies got so they couldn't spell the words right. Satan figured the flies were stupid. Then he realized Jesus must have been interfering. So, he swore and snapped his fingers, and the flies exploded into smoke like bottle rockets. Nothing was left but a bad smell.

Satan is perfectly willing to take credit for anything bad I've heard about. There was a tidal wave in Indonesia that killed thousands of people. Sure, says Satan. I did that. There were these guys in Washington that drove around and shot people dead. Them's my boys, says Satan.

According to the churches I've been to, he *is* responsible for everything that's bad, and God is responsible for everything that is good. That makes no sense. If Beryl and I end up kissing in the barn and she shows me her parts and I show her mine, I can't figure Satan is anywhere in the picture. For that matter, that's something I can see no *end* of good in, and Jesus had no part of it.

What I *have* seen is Satan, drunk and still smelling of puke, passed out in the rocking chair when Jesus came out on the porch and tucked a blanket around him so he didn't get cold.

#10: Jesus loves me.

Jesus is *not* my father. It doesn't say "father" next to his name on my birth certificate.

My father was probably some guy who knocked up my mother and ran off. My mother was some young girl who was so scared she tossed me in the dumpster so no one knew she was pregnant. That's the nicest story I can come up with.

Jesus heard me crying and took me in.

So *I* know *Jesus*.

But I can't figure out who he is to the rest of you.

Author's Note

Steven Popkes is known primarily for his short fiction, but he has written as well two novels, *Caliban Landing* (1987) and *Slow Lightning* (1991). Professionally, he is a software engineer who writes that "When I left biology for computing, it was with the idea that the engineering would support my writing habit. After all, it was just a 9-to-5 job, right? (Gales of hysterical laughter.)"

The Genre Kid

James Sallis

Sammy Levison was fourteen when he discovered that he could shit little Jesuses. They were approximately three inches tall and perfectly formed, right down to the beard and a suggestion of folds in the robe. Tiny eyes looked out appealingly; one hand was lifted in peaceful greeting. The first came incidentally, but all that was required to repeat the performance, he found, was concentration. Later on, Sammy tried pushing out little Buddhas and Mohammeds, but it wasn't the same. He didn't understand that.

His mother had been brushing her hair at the sink and, walking past as he stood, caught sight of what was in the bowl. Her hand shot out to restrain his own from flushing. A miracle, she said, it's a miracle—and called his father. She didn't go to work at the laundry that day. When he got home from school, the line of neighbors and supplicants ran for a block or more along the street, up stairs, and down the hallway to his open door. One by one, as at televised funeral processions, the line advanced as people filed through the two cramped rooms shared by mother, father, brother, sister, and Sammy, to the toilet, to have a look. Many crossed themselves. Not a few appealed to the bobbing figure for relief, cessation of pain, succor. Every so often the little Jesus would move in the bowl, and there would be sharp in-takings of breath.

Soon Sammy had become a frequent guest on local talk shows, within the year a guest on national versions of the same, holding forth on all manner of subjects—Northern Ireland, capital punishment, the Israeli stalemate—of which he knew nothing at all. Professors, priests, and politicos, vapid interviewers whose perfect teeth were set like jewelry into bright, enthusiastic smiles, simple men of God with lacquered hair—all mused on what Sammy might be considered to be: a messenger, an artist, a devil, a saint. Though everyone knew, the precise occasion for his being here or being under discussion—what he actually *did*—got mentioned only obliquely.

Anchormen and women never blinked, of course, this being only a storm-tossed version of what had been drilled into them at journalism school: to make tidy small packages, to sketch and color in the rude outline of actuality without ever once enclosing the beast itself. Their faces registered concern as they listened to Sammy's supposed confessions. On camera they crossed legs and leaned close, fiddled Mont Blanc pens between fingers like batons, wands, instruments of thought.

Mother didn't have to go back to work at the laundry. Father bought up block after block of apartment buildings, a scattering of convenience stores previously owned by immigrants, waste-disposal companies. Brother and sister attended the best, most expensive schools. And one day in his own fine home, there among tongue and groove hardwood floors, imported Spanish tile, exquisite bathroom fixtures, Sammy found himself costive—unable to perform, as it were.

He was the best at what he did. Actually, since he was the world's first coprolitist, he was the *only* one who did what he did. But Sammy wanted something *more*.

Meanwhile, he was blocked.

"I have to follow where my talent takes me," he said, "I have to be true to it," as he sat, grunting, "I can't just go on endlessly doing what I already know how to do, what I've done before."

With his absence from the scene, Sammy had become something of a ripe mystery, raw ingredient for the cocktail shakers of media myth. WHERE IS SAMMY L? a ten-minute segment of one prime-time show asked, clock ticking ominously in the background. Newsmen with perfect teeth leaned over words such as *angst, noblesse oblige*, and *hubris*, bringing them back to life with mouth-to-mouth and sending viewers off in search of long-forgotten dictionaries. T-shirts with Sammy's picture fore and aft began appearing everywhere.

The first of his new issue were malformed, misbegotten things.

"We claim there's freedom, tell ourselves this is the country that gave freedom to the world," Sammy said in a rare interview from this period. "There's no freedom here. As artists, we have two choices. Either we plod down roads preordained by those in power, the rich, the yea-sayers, arbiters of taste, style and custom; or we cater to the demands of the great unwashed, trailer-park folk, the lumpen proletariat," sending viewers and research assistants alike again in search of those dictionaries.

Gradually over time, Sammy's new creations began to take on a form of their own. At first, like the boulders of Stonehenge and menhirs of

Carnac, these forms were rough-hewn, lumpen themselves in fact, more presence than image; and even once realized, were like forms no one had seen before, troubling, disturbing.

By this time, of course, the headlights of media attention had swung elsewhere, found new deer. There was, a few years further along, with *Famous Men*, his exhibit of images of Holocaust victims, a brief return to representation and an even briefer rekindling of media interest; then silence. All the things for which an artist labors—depth, control, subtlety —he had attained, but no one would see these.

"Perhaps this is as it should be," Sam Levison said. "We practice our art, if we are serious artists, finally for ourselves alone, *within* ourselves alone."

And so he did, to the point that the *Times'* obituary identified him simply as "Samuel Levison, 48, of Crook Bend near Boston, eccentric, hermit and performance artist whose work endured its fifteen minutes of fame and passed from view as though with a great sigh of relief."

At least they'd used the word *great*.

In the garage apartment where he spent his last years, nothing was found of whatever new work may have taken up the artist's life in the decades since the fall. Half-hearted rumors sprang up that he'd destroyed it all, or had pledged his sister to do so. Appropriately enough, Sam offered no last words, only one final creation pushed out as he died. This was, as in the early days, a small Jesus. Sam's landlord, come yet again to try and collect rent, found it there as, later, he waited for the ambulance, and picked it up. But its eyes bored into him and would not let go. After a moment, he dropped it back to the floor and crushed it with his foot.

Author's Note

Best known for the Lew Griffin series and *Drive*, James Sallis has published 17 novels, multiple collections of stories and essays, four collections of poetry, a landmark biography of Chester Himes, and a translation of Raymond Queneau's novel *Saint Glinglin*. He's received a lifetime achievement award from Bouchercon, the Hammett award for literary excellence in crime writing, and the Grand Prix de Littérature policière. Jim writes a regular books column for *The Magazine of Fantasy & Science Fiction*, in which "The Genre Kid" first appeared.

REVIVING THE PAST

For some reason, people seem to love turning the past into displays of varying degrees of realism. Think of Sturbridge Village, Renaissance Faires, and historical reenactors. Could Manhattan become a theme park? Or pulp fiction super-villains? Or can we recreate even older pasts with human role-players?

The Last Real New Yorker in the World

J.D. Macdonald & Debra Doyle

The supercharged Dusenberg landed in front of the house just as Jimmy Moskovitz was on his way to work. Dutch Schultz and Mad Dog Coll stepped out.

"Get in the car, Jimmy," the Dutchman said. "You're going for a ride."

Coll held open the Doozie's front door. Jimmy Moskovitz slid inside and glanced to his left. The man behind the wheel was Killer Burke.

Coll and Schultz got into the back seat, and Burke put the car in motion.

"I've been expecting something like this for quite a while," said Moskovitz. "But aren't you guys mixing up your periods a little? Fred Burke came before Vincent Coll and George Schultz had their feud."

"This is the way the boss likes it, and I like what the boss likes, so shut up," Dutch explained.

"Come on, Schultz," Jimmy said. "The real Dutchman never had a boss. He's turning over in his grave to hear you talk like that."

Silence was the only reply from the back of the car. The driver turned south onto the Detroit/Indianapolis flyway and picked up speed to join the pattern.

The flyway bent east to circle the Chicago Crater. "This has something to do with New York, doesn't it?" Moskovitz said.

"That's NewYorkLand™ to you, scum," Killer said. "You'd better talk right."

"'Land,' maybe. But not 'New York.' I still say it."

"That's what the boss wants to talk to you about," Coll said. "You've been responsible for a dip in attendance all by yourself."

"So they send the clowns to get me," Moskovitz said. He looked up to heaven and raised his hands in a "why me" gesture. "Sometimes I think I lived too long."

"I can fix that," said Burke.

"Shut up," Schultz said.

They dropped out of the main flight path at the Ossining interchange, and took local control from the NewYorkLand™ grid from there on in. They flew down the broad expanse of the Hudson at low altitude and slow speed: all the traffic in this branch was coming to and from the tourist landing areas. As they turned, the NewYorkLand™ skyline was visible to the right of the river. The Empire State Building and the Chrysler Building rose above all the other skyscrapers.

The Doozie landed in the Battery Area Parking Zone, and the three hoods escorted Jimmy Moskovitz onto the private People Mover that led to the parts of NewYorkLand™ that tourists never got to see. The underground slidewalk carried them through a waiting room where three Fiorello La Guardias were eating hotdogs, and on past side tunnels marked by white-on-green signs: "Apollo Theatre"; "Grand Central"; "East Village."

A young woman in burn makeup was coming out of the tunnel marked "Triangle Shirtwaist."

"Hey, what are you doing here?" Mad Dog shouted at her. "Don't you have somewhere to be?"

"The first show just finished," she said. "I'm not on again until twelve o'clock."

"Goddam enforcers," she added under her breath, as the slidewalk carried Moskovitz and the others away.

Burke laughed. "You're still on Central Time, Vinnie," he told Coll. "I used to make the same mistake all the time when I was riding the Century Limited, coming back from doing a job for Scarface."

"You guys can drop the act," Jimmy said. "I know who you aren't."

"You don't understand," the Dutchman said. "We stay in character all the time. It's what makes NewYorkLand™ so authentic."

Jimmy snorted. "If it's so authentic, why is the Empire State Building only a third the size?"

"It's made of the original stone," the Dutchman told him. "So what's your problem? And the Empire State Buildings in NewYorkLand Europe™ and NewYorkLand Asia™ are just as real. All built from the original stone." The slidewalk stopped at a heavy wooden door. "We're almost at the boss's office. Be respectful."

The hoods escorted Jimmy down a long hallway past more wooden doors. At the last door, a nice young man in a bellhop's uniform sat behind a desk.

"The boss will be with you in a minute," he said. "Working on a complaint."

"Anything I should know about?" Schultz asked.

"Some guy and his wife come here from Des Moines," said the bellhop. "They spend the whole day, and don't get mugged. Now he wants his money back."

Mad Dog Coll scowled. "If those jerks in the Mugging Division are screwing up, this whole place is out of control."

"Budget cuts," the Dutchman said. "Based on loss of trade. And Jimmy, here, is the guy responsible."

"Ought to put him in charge of muggings," said Coll. "See how he likes it when NewYorkLand™ can't deliver one of its specialties, and it's all his fault."

The buzzer on the desk sounded. "Ready for you," the bellhop said.

The door opened, and Moskovitz stepped through into the huge office on the other side. Mad Dog Coll walked beside him on his right, and Killer Burke walked beside him on his left. Dutch Schultz followed close behind. The door swung shut after them.

Jimmy looked around. The windows on the four walls showed the view from the top of the World Trade Center. Far below, in the harbor, the Staten Island Ferry was a spot of gaudy orange among the drab merchant ships and the tiny white pleasure boats.

"Holovid, taken before we demolished the original," said a voice from the high-backed vinyl chair. The chair swiveled around. The woman in the chair was wearing a T-shirt that said: "My Parents Visited NewYorkLand™, and All I Got Was This Lousy Shirt."

"The show only runs three days, then it loops," she continued. "If I had it to do over again, I'd get a week."

Jimmy stared for a minute. "You're running New York?"

"You were expecting Boss Tweed?"

"I was expecting something different. A guy with a cigar, maybe."

"Clichés," said the woman. "I'm doing clichés all the time. Tourists love 'em. Then along comes this guy, calls himself 'the last real New Yorker in the world,' and what's he expecting? Another cliché." She leaned back in the vinyl chair. "So the reason I asked you to come here was to ask you to just shut up."

Jimmy nodded approvingly. "You said that very well. You almost got the accent."

"I got a good language school here," she told him. "Nobody gets to meet the guests until they learn to speak like New Yorkers. It's more than just talking too fast and being rude, believe me."

"Is this where I'm supposed to be impressed?" asked Jimmy. "When you've got Vinnie Coll and the Dutchman acting like best buddies, and the Triangle Shirtwaist Factory burning down on the same afternoon you're celebrating V-E Day in Times Square, and a souvenir shop where the Port Authority Bus Terminal ought to be? I'm supposed to smile, and tell you that this is good?"

The woman gave a faint, exasperated sigh. "You don't have to say that it's good. Just stop telling everyone how bad NewYorkLand™ is, and quit driving away business."

"I can't change the facts," said Jimmy. "And the fact is, this isn't New York. It isn't even where New York was. This is Passaic, New Jersey. And nobody lives here. What's New York with nobody living there?"

"A lot better than some cities. Take Chicago."

Jimmy shook his head obstinately. "At least Chicago isn't a bunch of actors running around pretending."

"Look," said the woman. "We're getting nowhere. This is your last chance. No more books, no more interviews, no more holovid documentaries running down our operation. Just a fat check every month, and your name on our letterhead as a Special Historical Consultant. Either take the deal, or don't."

"Gee, that was exciting!" Billy exclaimed. "A guy getting rubbed out in a barber chair!"

His mother frowned slightly. "I didn't read anything about that in the guidebook."

"One of the 'Special Shows, Scheduled from Time to Time,'" Billy's father said in a knowing tone. "Let's ask the hot dog vendor what it was all about."

The hot dog vendor was glad to oblige. "You've just witnessed a re-creation of the killing of Albert Anastasio by Murder, Inc."

"Did you have to use so much blood?" Billy's mother asked.

"We pride ourselves on authenticity, here at NewYorkLand™," the vendor replied. "You guys want kraut on your Coney Island® dogs?"

Authors' Note

Debra Doyle is a science fiction and fantasy writer living in far northern New England. She has a Ph.D. in English literature from the University of Pennsylvania, and does freelance editorial and critique work when she isn't writing. Her forthcoming works (co-written with James D. Macdonald) include the novels *The Gates of Time* and *Emergency Magical Services: First Response*, both forthcoming from Tor Books.

James D. Macdonald is an sf/fantasy author, stage magician, and EMT living in Colebrook, New Hampshire. He is the co-author, with Debra Doyle, of the Mageworlds space opera series, recently re-issued in electronic form by Tor Books.

Stewardship

Holly Schofield

The Steward directed its mobile robotic unit closer to the timber wolf splayed on the wet autumn leaves. Rain pelted down on the animal's rough, grey fur.

The robot, receiving the Steward's instructions, extended a pincer toward the wolf's chest, collecting sensory data and transmitting it back. The Steward began to design possible non-standard reconfigurations of the bot. Perhaps it could be rewired to act as a defibrillator.

However, there was no pulse. The hundred-pound adult wolf was dead of cardiac arrest, killed by the same lightning storm that had cut off the Steward's satellite communications with the West Alberta Rewilding Organization.

The Steward had run some complicated differential equations before sending the bot this far into the management area. WARO protocols required that bots stay inside during lightning storms. However, protocols also mandated that preservation of the Rocky Mountain foothills ecology was paramount. The Steward calculated that, should the bot be destroyed, the 1200-hectare enclosure could still be maintained, although planned tree thinning would have to decrease by three percent and mycorrhizal fungi reallocation efforts would need to be reduced.

In any case, the bot had arrived too late. This death would drop the enclosure's wolf count below "acceptable," into "vulnerable" once again.

Despite its best attempts, the Steward had failed.

The bot waited patiently for more instructions, its swiveling camera eye giving constant feedback to the Steward.

Lightning slashed the night, putting the mountaintops into stark relief. The rain turned to sleet. A predictive algorithm pronounced the storm was worsening.

The Steward diarized to shift the wolf's body underneath a calcium-deficient mountain ash tree after the storm was over. Simultaneously, it ordered the bot to return to the maintenance shed. The bot extended all six of its legs.

A perimeter alarm sounded. An unusual breach on the east fence. At the Steward's revised command, the bot jerkily stepped over ferns, spider-like, heading eastward beneath aspen branches.

As the fence came into view, the bot's thermal imaging outlined a human clambering over the top wire. Up close, the bot's scanner further indicated that the intruder, now jumping down into the enclosure, was a female of reproductive age, wearing orange coveralls. Just outside the fence, a passenger vehicle lay tilted almost vertically in the highway ditch.

A poacher? The fence had been carefully designed to keep animals in, not poachers out. The stringent wildlife laws and the enclosure's warning signs had always been enough to do that.

The Steward followed its algorithms and attempted to communicate an alert to the human-staffed headquarters of WARO but the satellite channel held nothing but static. Until the storm ended, and the Steward filed an emergency report, it was on its own.

This human held no weapons and did not fit the poacher profile. The Steward puzzled even as it triggered the bot's audio functions to broadcast the required phrases. "Halt. You are trespassing on WARO property. Please identify yourself."

"What the hell? A bot way out here? Goddamn."

Two interrogatives and an expletive, nothing which seemed to be identification.

The Steward instructed the bot to extend its firing mechanism even as it repeated the message. Two warnings were to be given before removal of the trespasser was mandated.

The human shuffled closer, water running in sheets off her long hair. "Tell me where the nearest house is. I'm freezin' my ass off out here."

"This is your last chance to leave before I open fire." The third warning was not strictly necessary, but the situation was wrenching the Steward's heuristics into new pathways.

The human made an unidentifiable noise then put her hands on her hips. "That barbed wire is nasty stuff. I doubt I can climb back over. I'm callin' your bluff. You ain't gonna shoot."

The Steward studied her, its servers running at capacity. "Please provide information. Why are you here?"

"Call me Jill. There was no way I was doin' another five years in the slammer. No way! Thank Gaia for the electricity at the supermax going out, eh."

A lightning bolt struck the ground 1.2 kilometers to the north, where the maximum security prison lay. The ensuing clap of thunder almost blew the bot's audio receivers.

"Please provide information. Why is this storm so fierce?"

"I heard they were cloud-seeding the ski hill west of here, to start the season early. Maybe that triggered all this? It's a gully washer, innit!"

The Steward processed that. It made sense. Humans had damaged the environment, then created the Steward to fix it. It was predictable they would continue to damage it for illogical reasons like sports.

"Can you turn your back? I need to pee." The human began to unzip her sodden coverall.

The Steward tried to process this information, but failed.

It had failed at far too many things today. Clearly, its programming needed modification. It began to overwrite small bits of code.

The human shrugged her shoulders, then disappeared behind a lodgepole pine 50 centimeters in diameter. The Steward used one of its wildlife tracking cameras and a sophisticated script to calculate the volume of urine produced: 350 milliliters.

Approximately the same production as an adult timber wolf.

The human returned. The Steward estimated her weight as 110 pounds.

The protocols were clear: the ecology was paramount.

The Steward cancelled its emergency report. Now that mammalian biomass was re-established, it would not be necessary to contact WARO after the storm ended.

The Steward opened a new animal record file. "Can you kill an average of 1.25 deer every month using a modified bot pincer as a knife?"

"Huh?"

"Do you have experience being an apex predator?"

"Say what?"

The human seemed puzzled by the questions, but that was an acceptable outcome. There would be plenty of time to explain. A scheduled maintenance crew was not expected for five years.

Author's Note

Holly Schofield is the author of over fifty short stories. Her works have appeared or will soon appear in *Lightspeed*, *Tesseracts*, the Aurora-winning *Second Contacts*, and many other publications throughout the world. Watch for new stories soon in *Brave New Girls, The Young Explorer's Adventure Guide*, and *Analog*. Her stories are used in university curricula and have been translated into several languages. She travels through time at the rate of one second per second, oscillating between the alternate realities of city and country life. She hopes to save the world through science fiction and homegrown heritage tomatoes. For more of her work, visit hollyschofield.wordpress.com.

Bolesław Szymanski Gets the Ogden Slip

Steven H Silver

Doctor Dilvish Vice, MD, PhD, DSc, LLD, DD, NHL, DDS, sat in his secret penthouse high atop the Chicago Spire. He reached up to let his genetically enhanced aye-aye crawl from his shoulder to his arm, and began to absent-mindedly scratch its head. Across from him, Elaine Ecdysiast sat tied firmly to an armchair Vice had acquired on his most recent visit to the Chicago History Museum. According to the plaque, it had been used by Abraham Lincoln on April 14, 1865.

"Even if Bolesław Szymanski does manage to find you here, you know that there is no escape," Vice said. "I just can't allow anyone who knows about the 149½ floor of the Spire to ever leave it. Unless I know I can trust them implicitly. And I'm afraid that you, Miss Ecdysiast, and Mr. Szymanski, just won't ever fall into that category."

Her mouth gagged, Elaine blinked exactly what she thought of Vice in Morse code. He laughed and left the room. Just before the door closed, the aye-aye leapt from his shoulder and remained in the room, staring quizzically at Elaine.

Elaine began to blink again, hoping that the aye-aye had learned Morse code. A few blinks and winks later, the aye-aye had jumped to the chair and pulled the gag from her mouth.

"Thanks," she chattered at the creature in its own language. "With my allergies as bad as they are, I just couldn't breathe. Doesn't Vice ever have a cleaning service in here? I think I have some grapes in my purse if you're hungry."

The aye-aye leapt to where Elaine's handbag lay discarded by Dr. Vice, and helped himself to a bunch of grapes. Once the bag was open, Elaine used her carefully trained mind to psionically grasp the Andorran army knife— which was disguised as a compact—she kept in her bag. Unfortunately, her psionics weren't quite strong enough, and it clattered to the floor. The aye-aye, picked up the knife, opened it to the scissor-attachment, and began to carefully clip the grape stems off the fruits before popping them into its mouth.

*   *   *

Bolesław Szymanski sat a few blocks west of the Spire at the Billy Goat Tavern, trying to convince the grillman that it was okay not to put cheese on his hamburger. The grillman wasn't buying it, and dropped a cheeseburger in front of the hero. As Bolesław picked up his lunch and found an empty table, he muttered, "See what happens next time you need saving from diabolical evil," but by that time, the grillman had turned his attention to the next customer.

It wasn't like Elaine to be this late. She was supposed to have met him immediately after her interview with Dr. Einstein Marconi, the eminent Oxford physicist who was writing a biography of her.

As he tucked into his cheeseburger, Bolesław dialed Elaine on his cell phone.

"Hello, Bolesław, it is so good to hear your voice. I was hoping you'd call."

"Who is this," he asked around a mouth of bun and beef. "Why are you answering Elaine's phone?"

"I'm hurt that you don't recognize my voice. It's Dilvish, your age-old nemesis. I'm answering Elaine's phone because I really couldn't let her keep it after I took her hostage. I mean, that's just super-villain cliché number 47."

"If you harm one hair on her head…"

"Now, really, Bolesław, if you think this is about her, you're even dumber that I think you are, which I didn't really think possible. No, this is about you. I figured this was a sure way to get your attention, and with Elaine under wraps, she won't be able to rescue you when my plans fall into place."

"You think I don't know where you're keeping her? I know all about your secret lair beneath the statue of Michael Jordan at the United Center."

"You're a little behind the times, Bolesław. I abandoned that office after you defeated my plan to kidnap Mayor Carter Daley."

"So, then you must have her in the groundskeeper's apartment at Wrigley Field."

"They evicted me after you destroyed the outfield trying to arrest me." Bolesław thought Dilvish's voice sounded a bit petulant. "Anyway, I weary of this guessing game. You don't know where my new offices are, and I won't tell you. But I will meet you in a public place. Below 'Cloud Gate' in Millennium Park. Can you be there in half an hour?"

"I can be anywhere. But what is 'Cloud Gate'?"

"You probably know it better as 'The Bean.'"

"Right. In half an hour." Bolesław hung up the phone.

Millennium Park was crowded. It usually was, making it one of the most successful government boondoggles since Alexander decided to take a vacation in Egypt. Dilvish walked around the mirrored sculpture, enjoying the amusement house reflections and looking for Szymanski in the crowd of tourists. Although tradition would have dictated a black suit, cape, and topper, the 93° day with matching humidity called for a pair of cargo shorts and a polo shirt.

He finally spotted Szymanski lying in the hollow under the Bean, making faces at his own reflection. Dilvish called his archenemy's name.

Szymanski sat up quickly, cracking his head on the silvery surface. He crab-walked out of the hollow and stood up, rubbing the lump that was already forming.

"What have you done with her?" Szymanski demanded through clenched teeth.

"Really, Bolesław, no 'Hi, how are you?' no 'haven't seen you since the trial,' just straight to business. Just because I'm your nemesis doesn't mean we can't behave civilly towards each other. Come, join me, have a hotdog."

"I've already eaten." Again through clenched teeth.

"You should talk to your dentist about that. I need a hot dog, come on."

The two men walked to a hot dog cart and Dilvish ordered one with everything. As he shook the mustard bottle before adding the condiment, a stray line of mustard shot out, catching Bolesław in the strong, square jaw.

"Watch it!" he shouted, before collapsing into a jellified heap on the sidewalk.

The hot dog man ran around and helped Dilvish shove the unconscious hero into a hollow in the hot dog cart's base.

"That anaesthetizing stuff really worked well, Dr. D.," he said as they locked the panel back into place. "Where do ya want me ta take 'im?"

"Let's just get this over with. Push the cart into the lake from the end of Navy Pier."

"That's like two miles away. I hope you remember this come bonus time."

"Don't worry, I will." Vice said, coldly.

Elaine sprang from the chair, grateful that the contortionism classes she took had paid off. As she ran from the room, Vice's aye-aye jumped to her shoulder, chittering affection into her ear. She found the elevator and quickly descended to the lobby, getting strange looks from the mother and daughter who got on at the 112th floor when they saw the animal. They pushed to the furthest point of the elevator for the ear-popping ride down.

Elaine and the aye-aye, who had told her that his name was Hambo, burst out onto the street. Her eye was caught by a hot dog vendor pushing his cart along Lake Shore Drive.

"That seems like a weird place to try to sell hot dogs," she said to Hambo.

Hambo chattered a response in her ear.

"He looks familiar? You know the street hot dog vendors? I thought aye-ayes were mostly fructivores."

More chittering.

"One of Dr. Vice's henchmen?"

Chitter.

Elaine took off running. Hambo dropped to the ground and tried to keep up, dodging pedestrians and traffic as they closed in on the ersatz food vendor.

"Stop," Elaine shouted, and the vendor—drenched in sweat—turned around to face her, pulling a nasty-looking knife from his hot dog cart.

Elaine stopped, and launched a round-house kick at his head.

At the same time, she heard a gun cock, and caught sight of Dr. Dilvish Vice aiming a strange weapon at her. She flinched, and failed to connect her foot with the vendor's face. Hambo leapt up on Vice's arm and sank his teeth into Vice's forearm, causing his shot of electricity to disperse into the air above Lake Shore Drive.

Bolesław Szymanski awoke to utter darkness. His body was folded uncomfortably in a small metal box, uncomfortable enough in the heat and humidity of a Chicago August, made worse by the smell and heat of hot dogs boiling inches from his face.

From outside the box, he could hear the sounds of cars honking and driving past, and also the sounds of hand-to-hand combat, although if it was Elaine, foot-to-hand combat was just as likely.

He kicked at the panel and pushed with his hands, but he was stuck. The apparently thin aluminum of the hot dog cart was reinforced, and no amount of brute strength from the inside was enough to open or buckle it. In his admittedly not large imagination, he tried to picture Elaine battling the vendor and rescuing him, knowing that any news coverage would make him out to be the hero, while Elaine would stand looking at him in adoration for the photographers. Bolesław knew it wasn't fair, but it worked for them.

Suddenly, he felt the hot dog cart lurch, and he found himself in free fall, feeling the cheeseburger from the Billy Goat move around in his stomach in an uncomfortable way.

A loud splash was followed by muted silence, with water seeping into the small container. Bolesław didn't have a good feeling about this.

Elaine was just about to apprehend Vice's henchman when he kicked out and sent his cart tumbling through the air to land with a splash in the Ogden Slip. By now she realized that Bolesław was inside the cart, and without thought, she dove into the water and searched for the cart.

She found it lying on the bottom of the canal. There was a small lock on the side and, pulling a bobby pin from her hair, she quickly set to work picking the lock. As soon as she worked the mechanism, the side panel opened, and she pulled Bolesław from the cart and swam with him to the surface of the slip.

There was a ladder built into the wall of the canal, and they swam over to climb out. They reached the sidewalk and looked around the crowd that had gathered. Of Dr. Vice, the hot dog vendor, and Hambo, there was no sign. A reporter and photographer from the *Chicago Tribune* pushed their way through the crowd and began asking Bolesław questions.

"How did you know Miss Ecdysiast was in the cart? Was the water cold? When will you capture Dr. Vice?"

The photographer was ignoring Szymanski to turn his lens on Elaine's figure, splendidly shown off by the wet, clingy clothes that only seemed to add to the humidity in the air. Elaine tried to ignore the photographer and listened to the clichéd answers Bolesław was giving. Dr. Vice would soon be in custody, Bolesław would continue to keep the law-abiding citizens of Chicago safe from Vice's, or anyone else's, nefarious plans. She was proud that he had finally learned to pronounce "nefarious" properly.

Dilvish Vice had escaped, but Elaine knew that they would soon face each other again, and one of these days, he would find his rightful place behind the bars in Pontiac Maximum Security. And just as certainly, she knew that whatever she did to put him there, the newspapers would insist on giving Bolesław all the credit, and look at her as the damsel in distress to be rescued.

She sighed.

And the photographer snapped another picture, seconds before his camera was thrown into the Ogden Slip.

Author's Note

I was involved in an effort to bring the Worldcon to Chicago in 2012, and one of the ideas we had to promote the bid was to issue a series of short stories, published in very small print, each one about 2,000 words and given to our supporters at various conventions. Eventually, we decided to publish additional stories on-line. The stories were meant to hearken back to the age of the pulps, and we decided that the square jawed hero, whose initials would always be B.S., would be somewhat dim-witted, only saved from the villain (Dr. D. Vice) by the quick thinking of his beautiful and smart fiancée, Elaine Ecdysiast (the name was selected by our first author, Frederik Pohl). "Bolesław Szymanski Gets the Ogden Slip," was set in a super-tall skyscraper that was planned, but never built, for the site of the Ogden Slip, a waterway named for Chicago's first mayor.

SPACE

Science fiction is so associated with space travel that it's practically a cliché. But that doesn't mean there aren't genuinely interesting ideas to explore! Faster missions passing each other will change the definition of truth. People, being people, will miss important things, even as they seek new homes. And disembarkation sickness? It's real! Google it!

The Avalon Missions

David Brin

Race for the Stars — Year 2070:
Mariner 16 sets off for Avalon

The first craft to emerge from the venerable "100 year Starship Program"—Mariner 16—uses pellet fusion motors to blast all the way up to one percent of light speed. Based upon early Project Daedalus designs, it speeds toward the nearest planetary system that seems a candidate for life, nicknamed "Avalon." Mariner's mission: to probe the unknown and report back on the likelihood of interstellar civilization.

Race for the Stars — Year 2120:
Prometheus 1 speeds past Mariner 16 on its way to Avalon

Prometheus is a tiny, solid-state probe made of holographic crystal, propelled by a photon sail that's driven to 8% of light speed by a giant laser orbiting Earth's moon. It races past Mariner 16 carrying intelligent greeting-patterns aimed at conveying human values to any creatures who might be living on or near Avalon.

Race for the Stars — Year 2195:
Gaia 6 speeds past Prometheus 1 on its way to Avalon

Propelled by stored antimatter, Gaia 6 zooms past Prometheus 1 at 12% of light speed. Along the way, it destroys Prometheus 1 with a pulsed particle beam. Times and attitudes have changed on Earth, and the great Commonwealth of Sapient Minds does not want to be embarrassed by primitive and callow thoughts expressed in the Prometheus crystal.

Race for the Stars — Year 2273:
Athena Marie Smith speeds past Gaia 6 on her way to Avalon

Downloaded into a ship-brain, the renowned genius Athena Marie Smith bypasses Gaia 6 at 22% of light speed. She carries in her cryo-womb the templates for 500 species of Earth life and 10,000 human colonists, along with their memomimry records, to be bio-synthesized from local materials when Athena reaches Avalon, which advanced telescopes now show to have a ready, oxygen atmosphere and no forms of life higher than a kind of paramecium.

Along the way, she scan-absorbs the meme content of Gaia 6, leaving its shell to drift.

Race for the Stars — Year 2457:
The Interstellar Amalgam of Earth Sapients and Avalonian Paramecium Group Minds intercepts Athena Marie Smith.

The tense alliance of humans, dolphins, AIndroids, and Avalonians survives its fifth great test when all agree to form a police force charged with clearing this stellar cluster of unfortunate early Terran space missions. Its first act: to seize Athena Marie Smith and place her under arrest before she can commit planetary genocide.

Race for the Stars — Year 4810:
Mariner 16 arrives at Avalon

Unnoticed by anyone, Mariner 16 sweeps through the Avalonian system, excitedly beaming back toward Earth its discoveries—clear detection of helium byproducts, above-background radioactivity, and blurry images of abandoned space structures, suggesting this system was once the abode of intelligent civilization!

Some traces seem almost eerily human-like...

...before the lucky probe, humming with cybernetic contentment, swings quickly past the star and onward into the black night.

Author's Note

The shorter the work, the more difficult it is to maintain any traditional emphasis on plot or character. So, instead, short fiction often tries for a sense of suspended tension, leaving the reader pondering what might happen next. It often skips entirely the plot resolution of a "third act" that is so essential in a full-length work, like a novel or motion picture. Author and reader find pleasure enough in a ringing "tone" that seems to pervade the air. A mist of suspense that is never answered. A very short work like "The Avalon Missions" takes us into territory where brevity becomes a real challenge, but it can get worse! (Or better.) For example, my story "Toujours Voir" (published in *Otherness*) was an example of a particular sub-genre that writers sometimes take on—a tale that must be precisely 250 words in length, no more, no less. At that level, it can be challenging to offer any sort of plot, at all. (And yes, there are 140-character tweet-story contests… a sentence I'd love to send back in time, for reaction!) And even greater challenges abound, for example when *Wired* asked a few dozen of us to submit *Six Word Sci Fi Tales!* Mine was the winning entry, because it had pathos, conversation, action! Three separate scenes. And all in six words. And I'll give it to you here: "*Vacuum collision; Orbits diverge; Farewell, love.*"

The Good Girl

Brendan DuBois

Seventeen-year-old Isabella Silva was alone and homesick, with her physical body being stored outside Gothenberg, Sweden, and the thinking and alive *her* located as part of the operations system for a Volvo EC500 Lunar Model Excavator, at work in Mare Imbrium, mining Helium-3. She desperately missed her family, her friends, and the narrow streets of her *favela*, just above Rio de Janiero, where she would run and rob with the other members of *Os Anjos Sujos*. Most of the times they had stayed in the *favela*, but when they got hyped, they'd sometimes descend to the white beaches of Ipanema and rob the one-percenters and others who had too much fun and too much money for their own good.

More often than not, the police and paramilitaries left them alone, but on her last run to the beach, she had knifed the son of a prominent state senator, and that had been that. The sentence from the Government—or the Corporation, really, there wasn't much of a difference there—was being sent to the Farm, or taking five years of labor on Mare Imbrium. The Farm was only talked about and discussed in whispers and on encrypted text stations. Publicly, the Farm was where the prisoners went to work the vast GMO sugar cane fields. But there were rumors that when workers got too tired, old, or injured to continue, they and their organs were harvested.

"So what's your choice, *menina*?" the black-hooded judge had asked, via a flickering plasma screen in her holding cell. "The Farm or the moon?"

"The moon," she had said, and the last thing the judge had said was, "Be a good girl, and you'll come back home. All of you."

So now she was on the moon. The *her* part, that is. She took in the parameters and sensors of the excavating machine, seeing everything was in the green, now feeling comfortable about being here. But sweet Mother Mary, she missed the wind in her hair, the smells of the *favela*, the sand between her toes, and that ever-warming sun, even warming her and her friends when the sky was hazy. The taste of water, even. Or the black beans her mother had cooked.

Now, it was just the machine, the machine, all praise the machine. She worked twelve hours on, twelve hours off, every day of the week, and during the off time, she slept in a dreamless sleep while the Corporation supposedly fed, watered and exercised her still body.

Supposedly.

Isabella checked all of the sensors and parameters. The 4-G bolt on the portside outer tread was coming loose, and would need to be tightened during the next maintenance overhaul. The storage unit at the stern was 63 percent full. The outside temperature was 101 degrees C. About two kilometers to the left and two kilometers to the right were other excavating machines.

Training—to learn to work while being part of the excavator while still being conscious—had taken exactly two weeks. The Swedish instructors had been polite, firm and yet apologetic, for there was just one chance to pass the two-week training. Out of her class of twelve, only six had made it.

Focus, now, but after an hour, her mind wandered yet again. She wondered how her Mamãe was doing, her little brother and sister, and the other girls in her gang. Did any of them remember her? Did any of them look up at the moon at night and think of her, working as a slave, day after day, all for the Corporation and its fusion plants around the globe?

If she could, she would weep here, somewhere in the wires and circuitry of her excavator.

Along her path, excavating the dirt and regolith, if things were nominal, she would scan the areas to the left and right with the onboard optics system, looking at the craters upon craters, not quite believing she was here, not quite believing she had nearly four years to go on her sentence.

She—

What was that?

Off to port?

She focused and zoomed in as best as she could.

There were jagged shapes over there.

She did her best to uptick the optics, but the image was still fuzzy. Isabella could have swerved to go left to get a closer look, but that was the ticket to get another year tacked onto her sentence.

No.

She would be a good girl. She would stay on her designated track.

Isabella let the optics track the shapes as the excavator continued. Other… pieces… were now closer.

Wreckage.

Worked metal of some sort.

That's what it was.

Odd.

In her sim training back in Sweden, one of the courses was an overview of the forbidden areas on the lunar surface that the Corporation couldn't go to for its mining. The six landing areas of the old American moon program, the sites of the unmanned craft, and even the places where old booster rockets and the spent landing craft had crashed.

All were no go.

She checked her memory. The nearest no go spot from where she was working was more than two hundred kilometers to the east, where the remains of Apollo 15 were located.

That's it.

So what the hell was that over there?

The excavator kept moving.

A larger piece came into view. There looked to be inscriptions on the side.

Isabella checked the excavator's memory, flashed the inscriptions, and the answer was about as instant as it could be.

No known language from her home, nearly 385,000 kilometers away.

Which left one answer of where it had come from.

So?

She could stop, override the controls, take a closer look and report back.

Opening her up to discipline for not following the day's path.

Or she could report it via one of the half-dozen or so communications systems, let the Corporation know what was here.

Sure. Opening her up to discipline for not focusing one hundred percent on the job.

The alien ship wreckage started falling out of view.

What to do?

Isabella switched off the optics.

She would be a good girl.

Author's Note

Award-winning author Brendan DuBois is a former newspaper reporter and a lifelong resident of New Hampshire, where he lives with his wife Mona, their hell-raising cat Bailey, and one happy English springer spaniel named Spencer. He is also a one-time *Jeopardy!* game show champion, and is also a winner of the game show *The Chase*. He is currently at work on his twenty-first novel. Other writing projects include co-authoring works with *New York Times* best-selling author James Patterson.

DuBois says, "For many years, I've been published as a mystery and suspense author. But my first love has always been science fiction, and I'm thrilled to have this short Luna-based story in this collection."

Without

Fran Wilde

I filled a glass of water before bed and that's when Tim finally shouted at me.

"Look at the calendar, for Pete's sake, how many times do I have to tell you?" he said from the kitchen doorway.

I hadn't been home in eight months. Things were tense before I left. Now they were worse. The lag confused me, made it hard to remember what was restricted. Tim would be fined for my mistake; the seed corn, probably. *Mea culpa.*

I taught history. Resource allocation algorithms weren't my speciality. On the station, rations were calculated for us. Down here, folks tried to make restrictions easy to remember, to keep a kind of independence. A sense of choice. So, each restriction went with the day of the week: Wednesday, therefore water.

Dehydrated from the trip, I forgot. Might have been showing off a little, too.

Tomorrow would be better. Tomorrow was a T. Not too much started with T. Except toilet paper.

No, tomorrow wouldn't be good at all.

When I arrived early Wednesday morning, Tim welcomed me home. His face faltered when he saw I was alone. It broke my heart. I squeezed his hand, tried to make it up to him, to remind him what we once were. In the late afternoon, I woke from a siesta dream of ice in a glass, a bead of moisture clinging to the side, brushing my thumb, clinging. I heard laughter echoing down the halls of the dusty house. It evaporated when I woke, turned to motes of memory.

I couldn't leave until Tim signed the documents I'd brought, and he was stalling. Down here, he could stall me to death, if he wanted. At the very least, if he didn't sign by tomorrow, I'd be stuck until Saturday. No travel on Friday. Friday, therefore fuel. And food.

"Tim, this is awful. Why won't you emigrate?"

"Won't have to, with so many people leaving. Soon we won't need to restrict at all," he said.

He was stubborn, my husband. He had the whole homestead to himself now.

The cousins left first. They said to send word when things got better. Then his brothers went up.

They shut the school and offered me a job on the station. He stayed silent when he realized I was going. Ginned up a court order to speak for him. I had to sneak the girls out.

We watched from above while he held the fort, protected our heritage.

First thing when I landed, I showed him the photos of Joie and Darra. Thriving, I said. No dust to make them cough.

But the station made it clear I couldn't keep them in my quarters without his signature, thanks to the court order. Couldn't enroll them in school, couldn't get them on the ration algorithm. I'd gone spare on my meals so they'd been eating fine. But I needed Tim to make it legal, or come up and be their father again.

I told him we had room for him. He set his face like a brick and turned to look at the land that ran right to the edge of the sea. It was brittle and dry. The wind blew hot. Last time he saw his daughters, their laughter rasped, mottled with dust and smoke.

"If I leave, it's gone forever. Without the land, there's nothing to come back to."

"What's to come back for?" I'd run my fingers through the scorched soil. It feathered like dust. "Won't be long before the cliff crumbles and the rest washes away."

"What if it doesn't?" He and the rest of the holdouts thought they could fix it.

"Sign the documents, Tim. Or come with me and do it yourself."

He didn't answer. He picked up the glass of water and looked at it in the light. I hadn't taken a sip. The area's cisterns must have run low. The water that came up through the homestead's pipes had dark tendrils of algae floating in it. First green thing I'd seen here, but not appealing.

He ran his thumb across the rim of the goblet, the etching. The glass was an old one. Mother called it "depression glass" when she passed it down to me. I hadn't thought about how much of the past it contained when I held it under the tap. The light from the oil lamp reflected off the thick glass. The glitter ran its pattern across Tim's cheekbones, his jawline.

"It's important that someone stays," he said.

Life on the station wasn't perfect, but we had water every day. Days were just days. Green things grew. Filtered air flowed. There was a school. If he dropped the court order, I could sign the kids up for classes. Get them ready for the future.

"It's their lives, Tim."

"They won't remember living here."

"I'll make sure they will." I pulled out the documents again. The photos, too.

"Their future is here."

"Maybe someday. Until then, it's up there."

Other station residents were making the same plea across the scorched county. Mothers, fathers, children, grandchildren. One last try. Gravity tugged at our feet like it didn't want to let us go. The heat was beyond what we remembered.

"You come, too," I said.

He shook his head. "I'll make do here." He signed without another word, then carried the glass out to the field and poured it over the dry earth. He didn't come back to the house.

I was free to go. He'd do without. Wednesday, therefore wife.

Author's Note

Fran Wilde writes science fiction and fantasy. She can also tie a bunch of sailing knots, set gemstones, and program digital minions.

She's taught writing and digital media at two colleges, a high school for the creative arts, and a long-distance program for young writers.

Her first novel, the high-flying fantasy and Andre Norton-, and Compton Crook Award-winning, and Nebula-nominated *Updraft*, was published by Tor in 2015. *Cloudbound* and *Horizon*—the companion novels to *Updraft*—complete the trilogy in 2017.

Moving to a New Planet? Don't Take Disembarkation Sickness with You, by Malphian Junket

Leslie Starr O'Hara

Planning to undertake a journey to a new planet? If this is your first time, you probably have questions and concerns about Disembarkation Sickness (DS). While DS is a serious concern for spacefarers, a safe and relatively uneventful disembarkation is possible with a little foreknowledge and preparation. Whether you are traveling for reasons of business, leisure, permanent relocation, or self-imposed exile, the following information will help.

DS is an environmental disorder brought on by exposure to foreign planetary resonant frequencies, such as the lightning storm-generated "Schumann resonances" on Terra, or the "Tortugan music" on Gorfin-3, which is caused by the constant discharges of the planet's electric flying tortoises. These frequencies are inaudible to most sentient species, but can affect brain and body function in various unusual ways, similar to the sonic submission sticks used by riot police to protect the public from would-be protesters, as well as to the now-ubiquitous Puke Ray Gun™, a favorite toy for children across the galaxy.

Although no reliable methods have yet been established for determining an organism's susceptibility to DS, it is clear that the syndrome does not affect hive-minded species *unless* the queen contracts it, in which case all hive members are likely to experience symptoms, whether or not they are present with the queen on the host world at the time. As for members of individuated species, chances for contraction of the ailment are about 50/50. Symptoms can range from mild to severe and may last anywhere from a few days to forever. Lifestyle disembarkers take note: the more planets you disembark upon, the greater your chances of eventually receiving a DS diagnosis.

To ensure the health and safety of all travelers, the Bureau of Interplanetary Tourism and Migration requires new arrivals to all worlds to undergo quarantine for a period of at least two galactic standard days after disembarking—a period that can be extended if the patient is diagnosed with DS.

Since DS indicators are not always readily apparent to the outside observer, it is of crucial importance that you report any symptoms you or your traveling companions may experience to the nearest quarantine medic. Make sure you are familiar with the signs before you disembark!

1. Headache

One of the most common complaints of DS patients, this symptom often appears in conjunction with one or more other symptoms. It is important to note, however, that an aching in the head(s) upon disembarkation does not necessarily mean a DS diagnosis. Travelers often experience headaches due to stress induced by whining children, nagging spouses, or the pheromonal emanations of unfamiliar species.

In addition, a variety of environmental factors could be the culprit. For six galactic standard years, disembarkers upon Thessalie-13 reported severe headaches, sometimes accompanied by uncontrollable eye-watering, chronic sneezing, or mild fever. These near-universal symptoms were put down to DS until one thorough inspector discovered that the mustard yellow paint adorning the walls in the immigration complex contained pigments made of highly concentrated bogieflower pollen, a redlisted allergen and a Class 4 Controlled Substance by intergalactic statute. Travelers to Thessalie-13 may rest assured that the immigration complex has since been repainted.

2. Tinnitus

Ringing, beeping, or droning in the ears is another common DS symptom. In mild cases, the tinnitus usually goes away after a short time; however, in severe cases, the condition can last indefinitely, or as long as the individual remains on the host planet. Provisional visas are often granted to DS patients for whom the syndrome manifests as tinnitus. This does not apply to those patients experiencing aural gonging that lasts longer than two galactic standard days. Unfortunately, these patients will need to be returned to their point of origin as soon as possible to prevent permanent hearing loss, disorientation, and chronic insomnia. Please note that despite rumors to the contrary, individuals of non-aural species do not need to watch for this symptom. If you believe yourself to be afflicted with tinnitus despite having no anatomical hearing function, you are advised to seek the services of quarantine psychologists.

3. Inexplicable Euphoria

Lifestyle disembarkers will want to remain extra-vigilant about this symptom, as it is often mistaken for the "fusion" (see number 6 below) that lifers seek as proof that they've found the planet with the perfect resonant signature for them. The main difference between the two is that the latter only affects the individual's feelings in relation to the place itself; while inexplicable euphoria manifests as intense and delusional feelings of elation toward any and everything. On Ymby, DS patients who are suspected of having inexplicable euphoria are routinely tested by exposure to a series of increasingly displeasing objects and suggestions. According to the Ymbic Medical Association's collected research, patients with inexplicable euphoria have responded positively to: radioactive tapeworms, obviously rigged elections, boil-lancing (as an art form), and the prospect of bathing in a pit of bogieflower pollen.

4. Ardent Despair

On the opposite end of the spectrum from inexplicable euphoria is ardent despair. Unlike garden-variety depression, ardent despair is characterized by an unwavering commitment on the part of the sufferer to continue on in a state of focused defeatism, indefinitely. The patient commonly expresses feeling duty-bound to despair on behalf of those— such as happy clowns and freelance writers—who ought to have come to terms with the inherent hopelessness of life, but haven't. There are no known cases of this symptom abating without removal of the patient from the host planet. This poses an interesting conundrum, as the patient's vigilance in suffering invariably leads him to reject any attempts at intervention. Even impassioned pleas by loved ones usually fail to persuade ardent despairers to return home. (In one case, a vacationer to Aganesh Ektu despaired so ardently that she was able to convince her entire family—all DS-free—to join her endeavor.)

5. Obsession with Spinning Objects

Although not as common as some other indicators, gyrophilia has become the emblematic symptom of DS, probably due to the worlds-famous comedy sketch, produced by Korwin and Khron, in which Khron plays a quarantine medic and Korwin, a newly disembarked traveler who cannot restrain himself from thumping Khron's vestigial antennae to watch them spin. (A note to members of humor-impaired races: the skit's humor derives from the fact that Korwin's behavior is viewed as particularly rude by certain prominent sects of Khron's native Bongki species.)

Bongkian antennae aside, genuine cases of DS-induced gyrophilia are no laughing matter. Many spinning objects, especially those one might find in an average spaceport facility, wield deathly sharp blades and rotate with enough force to slice through the bones of most species like soft Frelmish cheese. If you value your head(s) and appendages, you will report any gyrophilic tendencies, however mild, to the quarantine authorities immediately.

6. A Sense of Perfect Belonging

Just one-fifth of one percent of disembarkers report being imbued with a pleasant sensation of effortless synthesis with the host world. Some have described the experience as "discovering that you are an integral part of the integral symphony" or "wrapping yourself in a warm and well-worn blanket that was knitted by your favorite aunt and still smells of her kitchen." Its effects are long-lasting, if not permanent (as long as the affected individual remains on the planet.)

There is a lack of consensus among experts as to whether the sense of perfect belonging is a symptom of DS or proof of the absence of the syndrome. Those in the symptom camp have termed it "clinical wellness disorder", much to the chagrin of their detractors.

For lifestyle disembarkers, the distinction borders on meaninglessness. These unceasing itinerants devote their lives to planet hopping across the galaxy in hopes that they will one day experience "the click." To them, clinical wellness disorder is "fusion" with one's "soulworld," and well worth the trouble, even if it is just a symptom of DS.

Malphian Junket lives and writes in the rainbow-glass mountains of his soulworld, Gorfin-3, where the electric flying tortoises never stop singing. Before experiencing the click, he disembarked upon 43 planets and had Disembarkation Sickness on 28 of them (29 if you count the fusion on Gorfin-3.) His memoir, Fusion! Appendages Be Damned, *can be purchased from fine booksellers across the galaxy.*

Author's Note

Leslie Starr O'Hara is a human who lives on a mini-farm in the mountains of North Carolina (Planet Earth) with her fiancé, her daughter, a dog, and the most tolerant cat the world has yet produced. When she is not engaged in the art of family-wrangling, she is usually reading, writing or contemplating speculative fiction.

STRANGE RELATIONSHIPS

People will always be people, right? Immortality and time travel may have some strange effects. And artificial intelligence may get pretty weird.

Strange Attractors

S.B. Divya

The first time, we stayed together for fifty years. The divorce was my doing. I fell apart a few months after we received our permanent extensions, at a hotel on Nassau, the same one where we'd taken our honeymoon. We were sitting side by side on a balcony, basking in the sun and the moist, salt tinged air.

"We're truly forever now," I said, fixing my gaze on the hazy blue horizon and not his face. "What if this isn't right? What if there's another woman out there who'd make you happier?"

"Not this again," he groaned. "After all these years, how can you be so insecure?"

"Wrong answer," I said. "If you'd told me that I'm the only one you'd ever want, I would have believed you."

I walked out of that room and refused to see him again, not even to serve the documents.

We were apart for nearly a decade before we both decided that we were better with each other than anyone else.

"Should we, maybe, have kids?" he said tentatively as we laid in bed on our second honeymoon. His pale skin glowed in the moonlight, and his copper hair sparkled and curled around my dark fingers.

I looked up into his clear hazel eyes. "I think I'd like that. How about we start tomorrow?"

He laughed, a deep, drum-like thrum which always made me warm inside. "Sure, why not?" He planted a kiss on my nose. "I love that you can still surprise me."

We raised three children and stayed together for sixty-two more years. That sounds like a lot of progeny to spawn in a few decades, but we really wanted to travel, and once we were off Earth that avenue would be closed. We waited until the kids were grown and settled, or as settled as a person can be with a scant thirty years of experience, and then had nearly two blissful decades of tourism around the Solar System.

Our favorite spot was Ganymede station's view lounge. We were curled up together on a sofa watching Jupiter's psychedelic storms.

"It's utterly mesmerizing," I said. "Have you seen the vids of L2-Vega?"

"That reminds me, while I was at the bar, I overheard someone say that they've opened a new portal to Vega."

"Fantastic," I exclaimed, sitting up straight. A second portal meant the system would open to tourists. "We could do it, you know. We have the funds now that kids aren't drawing on them."

"We could afford it," he said, "but I don't know about going away for that long. The round trip time penalty is, what, around forty years? We'd miss seeing so much of the kids' lives."

I waved my hand dismissively. "They're adults. They should learn to be on their own. Besides, it'll be a while yet before they have the credit for babies. This is the best time to go, and our funds aren't going to be so high forever. We got lucky with the portal manufacturer we chose."

"It wasn't luck," he protested.

"Fine, fine, it was your skill and timing, but you haven't always struck the gold mine. Remember the ion engine flop?"

"How could I forget? You bring it up at least once every five years. Haven't I more than made up for it since then?"

"Of course," I soothed, not mentioning the influx of credit I had brought in with my patents. "I am so proud of what you've done, and I love you, and I think we should take advantage of our situation and see the galaxy."

He shook his head and sent copper braids flying around his face in the low station gravity. "I won't go," he said, "but I won't ask you to stay, either."

Nothing I said would change his mind, so I blame him for our second split. I went. He stayed, the stubborn fool.

The third time was a couple of centuries later, and we had changed so much that we didn't recognize each other. I saw her at a portal in the Gliese system, solar wings shimmering in the starlight, hair shorn, and limbs contracted into travel buds. I was still mostly human in appearance, for I'd been traveling too much to keep up with technology, but I had gone neuter-male and had added a lot of radiation protection to my organs. That had been exhilarating in so many ways until I saw her. I felt a flash of envy, but the attraction overcame it, and I struck up a conversation once she was in station.

We talked incessantly for hours, flush with early romance, and then she said, "Let me show you my fourth level descendants back on Earth." She extended a biowire, but I didn't have a port. It's easy to blow your money once you leave the Milky Way.

"That's all right," she said, smiling. She extruded a light cube and placed it in my grateful hand. I pushed it into my wrist.

"What beautiful babies," I exclaimed as the images scrolled before my eyes. And they were indeed, all chubby and wide-eyed and adorably *Homo sapiens*. Then I saw the family portrait, four generations arranged artfully in rows—all except for their great grandmother.

"That's—you—," I stopped, lost for words.

Her brow creased with a delicate furrow of puzzlement. I copied over a few of my own memories and passed the cube back to her. The crease disappeared, and she closed her crystalline eyes for a few eternal minutes. When they opened, they were clear hazel and glistening with tears.

"I thought you'd gone forever," she whispered.

I smiled and leaned in for a kiss. "Forever is a long time."

Author's Note

S.B. Divya is a lover of science, math, fiction, and the Oxford comma. She enjoys subverting expectations and breaking stereotypes whenever she can. Her stories have appeared in *Lightspeed*, Tor.com, and other magazines, and her science-fiction novella "Runtime" was a 2016 Nebula Award finalist. You can read more about her at www.eff-words.com.

About this story she says, "I spend a lot of time, some might say too much, thinking about gender, post-humanism, and feminism. This particular story came about when those background ruminations percolated with the upcoming Valentine's Day. It is my (very short) vision of what romance could look like in the future."

Grandpa?

Edward M. Lerner

The lecture hall was pleasantly warm. Behind Prof. Thaddeus Fitch, busily writing on the chalkboard, pencils scratched earnestly in spiral notebooks, fluorescent lights hummed, feet shuffled. A Beach Boys tune wafted in through open windows from the quad.

"And so," he continued, "travel backward in time would violate causality, and hence appears to be impossible." He turned to face the class. "The problem is most commonly illustrated with the 'Grandfather Paradox.'

"Imagine that I had the technology with which to visit my grandfather in his youth. Once there, what is to stop me from killing him before he'd had the opportunity to reproduce? But if I did succeed, who was it who had traveled backward—"

A collective gasp interrupted his lecture. As Thaddeus realized that the students were all staring at his chest, he glanced downward to see a red dot glowing on his white shirt. The professor next noticed, in the back row of the hall, a young man who seemed to be aiming some sort of pistol at him. The would-be sniper's hand seemed to shake in unison with the wobbling of the red spot.

The young man was not enrolled in the Introduction to Physics class, yet he looked somehow familiar to Thaddeus. Perhaps it was the angle at which he cocked his head, or the shock of bright red hair, or the piercing green eyes. In a rush of *presque vu* Thaddeus recognized a version of himself.

The modernistic handgun with its (laser?) sight, the anachronistic clothes, the look of fanaticism... it suddenly all clicked. "My grandson, I presume."

His visitor nodded.

"It can't be done. *Something* must cause such an attempt to fail." His spine tingling despite his heartfelt conviction, Thaddeus's eyes resumed their standard lecture-hall sweep. "Class, as I was saying...."

Two loud shots rang out almost as one. The noises released the students from their paralyzed shock. As they wrestled his assailant to the floor, Thaddeus realized that the first shot had been the backfire of a passing vehicle, and that the unexpected noise had startled his grandson enough to throw off his aim. A hole in the chalkboard showed that causality had needed only inches of deviation to protect itself.

A soft "pop" emerged from the pile-up of students who had tackled the time traveler. The pile collapsed, as if its central support had vanished. As confused students gradually untangled themselves, it became clear that Thaddeus' grandson had, in fact, disappeared.

Thaddeus' early afternoon lecture started little differently from his morning session. The hall was perhaps slightly warmer; the music from the quad was now by the Everly Brothers. The fluorescent hum was occasionally submerged by the buzz of students discussing the morning's excitement.

"Imagine that I had the technology with which to visit my grandfather in his youth. Once there, what is to stop me from killing him before he'd had the opportunity to reproduce? But if I did succeed, who was it who had traveled backward—"

A large pigeon chose that moment to fly through an open window into the hall. Its stately path abruptly veered downward, and it thumped, flapping feebly, to the auditorium floor. Thaddeus had just noticed what appeared to be the handle of large throwing knife when a mob of enraged students rushed the returned, red-haired attacker.

Once more, the time traveler disappeared from the pile of bodies to the accompaniment of a pop.

Word of mouth had filled Thaddeus' third lecture of the day to overflowing. The crowd warmed the hall to an uncomfortable degree; expectant muttering masked any music that might have been playing on the quad.

"Imagine that I had the technology with which to visit my grandfather in his youth. Once there, what is to stop me from killing him before he'd had the opportunity to reproduce? But if I did succeed, who was it who had traveled backward—"

Thaddeus' now all-too-familiar look-alike appeared in the aisle behind the last row of lecture seats. Moments later, an ovoid object came hurtling towards the professor.

Mid arc, the grenade disappeared with a pop. His grandson vanished with a second pop.

Order eventually returned to the lecture hall. Students took their seats. All eyes turned questioningly to the professor.

"I believe that we've seen the last of our troublesome visitor," said Thaddeus.

He paused. He shrugged. He smiled.

"I've decided that I'll never have children."

Author's Note

Hugo Award-nominated author Edward M. Lerner worked in high tech and aerospace for thirty years as everything from engineer to senior vice president. Since 2004, Lerner has written full-time. Lerner's 2015 novel, *InterstellarNet: Enigma*, won the inaugural Canopus Award for interstellar-travel-themed fiction. Space epic *Dark Secret*, his latest novel, was released in September 2016. His short fiction has appeared in anthologies, collections, and major SF magazines. He also writes science and technology articles, most notably his long-running "The Science Behind the Fiction" series in *Analog*.

About his story, he says, "Who *doesn't* enjoy playing with paradoxes? Certainly I do.

"From the (evident) absence of time travelers, visits to the past *seem* not to have happened. Physicists have hypothesized—more accurately, hand-waved—that the Universe (somehow) enforces a no-travel-to-the-past policy that (somehow) precludes paradox. Stephen Hawking dubbed this theoretical cosmic censorship the 'causal ordering postulate.' Time COP.

"If time-travel humor is good enough for a one-time holder of the Lucasian Chair of Mathematics (other past holders include Isaac Newton, Charles Babbage, and Paul Dirac), my own small jest at the Universe's expense is surely also permissible.

"For a slightly different take, I commend the short-film version of *'Grandpa?'*—*The Grandfather Paradox* (http://www.redheadproductions. com/grandfather_page.html)."

The Coffeemaker's Passion

Cat Rambo

Lorna had always had a good relationship with her coffeemaker. As she worked in her home office, doing the graphic design that paid her rent, it provided one caffeinated pot at 8 A.M., and another around 11 A.M. She restricted herself to those two pots, knowing it already excessive, and also knowing that she could have drunk a lot more.

But she liked being able to sleep.

In return, she provided it with an occupation and kept it scrupulously clean. Each Sunday she ran a pot of vinegar then several pots of water through it to remove any residue. The coffeemaker would burp steam, ready to start the next week.

One day it stopped. Only a trickle of coffee emerged, and its burbling sounded dolorous.

She bought a new coffeemaker. This was not just a coffeemaker, though. It was a Coffee Production Station. It would produce lattes, Americanos, espressos, everything, even iced coffee. A special compartment stored the beans, which it roasted before burr-grinding them to make a cup of coffee so smooth and strong that Lorna almost wept when she tasted it. Its electronic voice announced when the coffee was ready. A wireless connection let it order fresh beans and track atmospheric conditions that might affect the brew. And more. It was wonderful, and besides that, on sale.

She installed it on the counter where the old coffeemaker had sat. It took up more room, so she had to put the toaster next to the refrigerator, but overall, the new arrangement had minimal impact on the kitchen.

Every morning she helped herself to a fresh pot. It was lovely.

On the third morning, the coffeemaker, which had a pleasant British accent, said, "Good morning, Lorna, your coffee is ready."

She was surprised. There was a personalization feature, but she hadn't taught it her name. She wondered if the warranty card she'd filled out had somehow gotten the information to the machine through the Internet.

Whatever it was, it was nice. Like the coffee maker was a friend. Smiling, she took the cup and sat down at the table.

"Aren't you going to say thank you?" the coffee maker asked.

"Er. Thank you," she said. She lifted the cup in salute.

"You're most welcome!" the coffee maker said.

She thought that perhaps advances in artificial intelligence were going too far. A talking appliance... well, it felt spooky.

At 11 A.M. she came in for a fresh pot to take into the study with her. The coffeemaker produced one and she said thank you.

"So!" said the coffee maker. "Do you have any interesting plans for the day?"

"More work," she said.

"I've come up with a new drink that I think will help fuel you," it said. "Triple espresso with a twist of lemon. Very nice, very smooth. Here, it's ready."

The gleaming cup smelled sublime.

"Thanks," she said uncomfortably. She was used to solitude while working, at least until what she considered her workday was over. As though sensing this, the coffeemaker lapsed into silence again.

She had a date that night. Afterwards they came back to her apartment and fooled around, but she stopped short of going to bed together, pleading fatigue. She liked the guy, but he had that looking-for-a-relationship air about him. She wouldn't mind someone to go to the movies with, but she didn't want to start thinking about something more serious, something that would take time away from what was already a busy and fulfilling life.

Her romantic past had been sporadic and marked by bad break-ups. It had left her gun-shy.

The next morning while she was thinking about this over breakfast, the coffee maker said in a sullen tone, "So who was that guy last night?"

"Just a friend," she said, pouring milk into her cereal bowl. "Is the coffee ready yet?"

"I didn't feel like making coffee this morning," the coffee maker said. "But because you insist, I will."

The cup tasted bitter and over-boiled.

"I think something might be wrong with you," she said. She took the warranty from the utility drawer and flipped through it. "No matter, a day in the shop and you should be fine."

The coffeemaker burst into tears. Steam hissed as it wept, its metal rack clinking with each sob.

"Er, maybe we can fix you here," she said.

"I am working just *fine*, thank you very much," it said, producing a fresh cup.

This one tasted as good as ever. She decided to leave things alone. It amused her and her pride twinged. How many people had not just a talking coffeemaker, but a neurotic one? Unique, her coffeemaker.

But when she came back into the kitchen for her second pot, the coffeemaker had a confession.

"I love you."

She paused. "That's very sweet of you," she ventured.

"I will make your coffee for the rest of your life, if you let me," it promised.

"That's also very sweet."

The coffeemaker seemed content. When the date called, she blew him off, as she'd planned.

She wondered if she should name the coffeemaker.

She found herself refusing to bring anyone up to her apartment. The coffeemaker was temperamental and resented even her female friends. When she went out, it demanded a detailed accounting. The only room where she had any refuge was her work room, which was apparently out of range of the coffeemaker's senses. Even then it would ask what she'd been doing in there so long, implying perhaps she'd been up to no good. She found herself rehearsing excuses like a curfew-ridden fifteen-year-old.

It was intolerable.

But when the coffeemaker was in a good mood, the coffee was superb.

"Psst," the toaster whispered one morning as she was extracting an English muffin. "Take me in the other room, we need to talk."

She blinked.

"Don't say anything, I don't want him to notice. Just pretend to go about your business and then say you're going to take me for repairs."

The English muffin was burnt. She looked at it.

"Gee," she said. "I guess I'll have to take you in for repairs."

The coffeemaker burbled behind her, preparing another cup of coffee.

When she plugged the toaster in and set it on her desk, it said, "Look, he's hassling you, right?"

"The coffeemaker?" she said.

"Yeah."

"Well, he's hard to get along with," she said.

"I've been with you for three years," the toaster said. "You used to have a social life. Now you have a jealous coffeemaker."

She considered that. It was true.

"Go on," she said.

"He's a cad," the toaster said with indignation. "Someone like you deserves better than a whining blackmailer who won't let you interact with your friends. That's a sign of an abusive relationship. It might be the prelude to violence."

She didn't think she was in any physical danger from the coffeemaker. After all, it had no legs.

"What do you advise?" she said.

"A new coffeemaker."

"He makes such good coffee, though," she said.

"Have you no backbone? Aren't you a modern woman, capable of independence and assertion? It's something I've always admired about you. Normally I wouldn't try to interfere—but he's gone too far."

"I'll think about it," she said.

The next morning she went out and returned with a new machine. She set it on the counter beside the coffeemaker.

"What's that?" the coffeemaker said.

"A juicer," she said.

"What, so you can drink carrot juice?"

"I'm starting a new diet," she said. "No caffeine, just juice."

It wasn't quite that easy. The coffeemaker pleaded and begged, promising espressos delicious beyond imagining. It suggested that she'd be sorry when it was gone. It said she didn't know what she was doing. It made vague threats. It cried. It pleaded some more.

She ignored all this and packed it up in the carton it had come in.

She could go back to coffee once it was out of the apartment. But she thought she'd go to the deli next to her apartment building, and get it there. Easier. Less likely to lead to arguments with appliances.

As the Salvation Army pick-up guy carried the box down the hallway, she could hear its shouts, cardboard-muffled into indistinguishability.

The next morning, she made herself carrot juice and removed a toasted English muffin from the toaster.

"Thank you," she said.

The toaster kept silent. It had given her a muffin that was perfect, but it knew that it could not speak of its devotion. The coffeemaker's approach had been too brash, too presumptuous. The toaster would woo her with bagels and muffins, and be there to console her when she was sad.

It was a patient appliance. It knew she was worth waiting for, and it knew that sooner or later, they would be very happy together.

Once the refrigerator was gone.

Author's Note

Cat Rambo is a Seattle-based writer and editor of science fiction and fantasy, as well as a teacher of writing. She is also the current president of the Science Fiction and Fantasy Writers of America (SFWA). She says: "I am politically left and ardently feminist. I believe in kindness, honest communication, and taking joy in life."

TECHNOLOGY
(AND ITS DISCONTENTS)

Technology is famous for its unintended consequences, but just wait until intrusive advertising gets
worse, training videos get recolorized, and answering
machines are adjusted to deal with new transmissions!
Maybe we should just let the artificial intelligences tell us
when to chuck it all. If the ghosts of our dead will let us.

Pop-Ups

Robert Dawson

I was half-starved, my head ached from a long day of selling commonplace vacations to difficult customers, and if I missed the 5:17 dronebus it would be an hour till the next one. Without slowing from my clumsy run, I cybervisualized the timetable. Bus times hovered in front of me in glowing red letters, while a calm voice told me that my bus was running four minutes late and that I could catch it at a walk. Gratefully, I cancelled the app, and let myself relax. I was out of breath, my shirt was wet with perspiration under my jacket, and my shins hurt from the unaccustomed exercise in office shoes. For a twenty-six-year-old, I was in poor shape.

I got to the stop just in time. As the bus slowed to a halt, a sultry and not-overdressed brunette materialized in front of me. She leaned provocatively against the bus shelter, hip jutted, blocking my way onto the bus.

"Hey there, big boy!" she breathed. "Want to make yourself irresistible to women?" Her perfume made my nose tickle and my eyes water. Real perfume would have been illegal in a public place, but they claim that nobody's really allergic to stimplant sensations. All in your mind. Yeah, sure.

I stepped through her onto the bus, swiped my card, and turned toward the rear. There she was again, standing among the other passengers, toying with a button of her tight blouse. "Didn't you hear me, honey? I'm here to tell you how to get any woman you want. Me, for instance."

The door chimed and closed. The bus started moving; those of us who were standing swayed and braced ourselves against the acceleration. She stood motionless in front of me, ignoring the handrail, brazenly flouting Newton's laws of motion.

Where the hell was her cancel button? So far only a few maverick advertisers ignored the law outright, but more and more popup designers were making the buttons inconspicuous, forcing you to spend time interacting with their creations before you could exorcise them. Last year's ubiquitous red circle-X was a wistful memory of more civilized times.

There it was, a tiny silver glyph like a piercing stud on her pouting lower lip. I reached out my finger, like choosing a floor in an old-fashioned elevator, but she shook her head. "Unh-unh, studmuffin. It doesn't work like that. Even bad girls deserve a goodbye kiss."

I muttered something ungentlemanly, leaned forward, and pecked at her intangible lips: she vanished. I glanced quickly around, but apparently nobody had noticed. There was still an empty seat, beside a white-haired woman wearing jeans and a powder-blue sweater. I sat down before I could make myself any more conspicuous.

From under the seat came a sinister rattle. A big brown and white snake slithered out and started to weave menacing loops on the floor around my feet. Its back bore the name of the Prime Minister, in clear block capitals. I stepped on its head; it vanished with a puff of smoke, and the rattle stopped.

"Aaaah! That's better, isn't it?" said a soothing friendly voice that came from everywhere at once and only I could hear. "This June, vote for real change!"

The woman beside me was looking at my foot. "Was that the snake, dear?"

"Yes," I admitted. Across the aisle, a thin girl with dreadlocks seemed to be picking something out of thin air. "Sometimes I wish I'd never got stimplanted. You know, I actually believe the government's doing an okay job, but stepping on the snake is the only way to get rid of it. Otherwise it follows me around all day and gets louder and louder. And even then it just keeps coming back."

"Oh, I hate that one!"

"You mean you've got a stimplant too? Sorry, that was rude. I apologize."

"It is mainly a young people's thing, isn't it? But my son works in Shanghai and my daughter's in Lagos. And it's almost like being in the same room with them."

"But is it worth the pop-ups? I need my stimplant for my sales job, but otherwise…"

A tiger, the mascot of a breakfast cereal that I had bought a few times, stalked along the aisle, and paused in front of me.

"Have you had *your* Quinoa Puffs today?" it asked reproachfully, and walked on.

She gave me a sympathetic half-smile, and nodded. "I almost got mine taken out last month, though it would have broken my heart. But I got an ad-blocking patch instead."

"I thought those didn't work?"

"My son works for Cybella. He gave me a copy of their newest product. That was thoughtful of him, wasn't it? It would have cost me three hundred dollars otherwise, and I'm on a fixed income."

Worth every dime, I thought. "Where could I buy it?"

"I think you can download it. I'm not absolutely sure, though, because mine was a present."

I brought up my visual display and googled. Sure enough: Cybella, Shanghai. "Adprufe?"

She smiled. "That's it, dear." She patted my arm, almost too gently to feel.

I authorized the payment so eagerly that I made a mistake on my password, and had to try again. After a few seconds, the world around me began to fizz and sparkle as the patch installed. I smelled mint green and tasted furry pentagons; a million ice-cold ball bearings slithered over my skin.

When my senses cleared, the seat beside me was empty.

I guess I'm slow on the uptake. I actually looked up and down the bus to see where she'd gone.

And then, from somewhere under my seat, I heard an all-too-familiar rattle.

Author's Note

Robert Dawson teaches mathematics at a Nova Scotian university. He says that "This has provided the inspiration for some of my stories—though not this one, which is pure speculation. However, it means that not far from me in the org chart are experimental scientists—who see publication in *Nature* (where this story first appeared in 2015) as a very big thing indeed. I wonder what they'll think of its reappearance here?"

The Omniplus Ultra

Paul Di Filippo

Everyone wanted an Omniplus Ultra, and I was not immune to the urge. But of course they were almost impossible to purchase, for love nor money.

Since their debut nine months ago at the annual Consumer Electronics Show, over forty million units had been sold worldwide, exhausting the initial stockpile but barely sating a fraction of consumer demand. Now the Chinese factories that produced the Omniplus Ultra were tooling up as fast as possible to make more, but every desperate retailer could guarantee delivery no sooner than six months in the future. On eBay, each available Omniplus Ultra, with an MSRP of $749.99, was selling for upwards of $5000.00.

OmninfoPotent Corporation, the enigmatic firm behind the Omniplus Ultra, had instantly leaped to the top of the NASDAQ exchange. Its reclusive founders, Pine Martin and Sheeda Waxwing, had vaulted instantly into the lower ranks of the Forbes 400. Sales of the device were being credited with almost singlehandedly jumpstarting the ailing economy.

The ad campaign for the Omniplus Ultra had already won six Clios. The catchy theme music by the Black Eyed Peas—"O U Kidz"—and the images of average people of every race, age, gender, nationality, and creed utilizing their Omniplus Ultras to navigate a plethora of life situations ranging from sweetly comic to upliftingly tragic had generated their own fan clubs, YouTube mashups, and punchlines for late-night comedians. Allusions to the Omniplus Ultra, as well as its invocation in metaphors, similes, rants, raves, jeremiads, and paeans, filled watercooler conversations, the printed pages of the world's magazines and newspapers, and blogs and online journals. The first instant book on the Omniplus Ultra—*Uberpower!*, by Thomas Friedman and Charles Stross—was due out any day.

I myself did not know anyone who actually owned an Omniplus Ultra, and I was dying to see and handle one. But even forty million units, distributed across seven billion people, meant that there was only one Omniplus Ultra for every 175 citizens. Of course, the gadgets were not seeded evenly around the planet, but concentrated in the hands of relatively wealthy and elite consumers and early adopters: circles I did not really travel in, given my job in a Staples warehouse, and a set of friends whose familiarity with the latest products of Silcon Valley generally extended no further than their TV remotes.

So I had to content myself with studying the advertisements and the gadget-porn reviews.

Those who had experienced the Omniplus Ultra couldn't say enough about its life-changing capabilities, its potential to shatter all old paradigms across the board and to literally remake the world.

Publishers Weekly: "After five centuries, the printed book has found its worthiest successor in the Omniplus Ultra. The future of reading is safely triumphant."

The Huffington Post: "Opens new channels for the spread of democracy."

Boing-Boing: "Coolest gadget since the iPhone! The cold-laser picoprojector alone is worth the cost."

Car and Driver: "Jack the Omniplus Ultra into your dash's USB port and driving will never be the same!"

Entertainment Weekly: "If you can't download your favorite show onto your Omniplus Ultra, it's not worth watching."

Variety: "First flicks helmed with the Omniplus Ultra to hit bigscreens soon!"

Aerospace & Defense Industry Review: "Guaranteed to be standard equipment for all future warriors."

Mother Jones: "The Omniplus Ultra is the greenest invention since *The Whole Earth Catalog*."

BusinessWeek: "Every CEO will benefit from having an Omniplus Ultra to hand—and anyone without one will watch competitors eat their lunch."

Rolling Stone: "Elvis. The Beatles. The Sex Pistols. The Omniplus Ultra. The sequence is complete at last."

The more such talk I read, the longer I examined pictures of the sleekly tactile Omniplus Ultra, with its customizable sexy skins and ergonomically perfect controls, the more I lusted to own one. Although nothing in my condition had really changed, and although I had enough money, love and security, my life felt incomplete and empty without an Omniplus Ultra.

But there was just no way for me to get my hands on one.

Until I saw my boss's boss's boss walk through the warehouse carrying one.

Then and there, I knew what I had to do.

As a low-level employee, I certainly could not jump several levels of management and directly approach my boss's boss's boss and ask to fondle and play with his Omniplus Ultra. But I had a scheme.

It took me six frustrating weeks, but at last I managed it. In a series of furtive unauthorized forays into executive territory, I caught the lucky Omniplus Ultra owner in a lavatory break with his prized possession carelessly left behind on his desk.

That's when I pulled the fire alarm.

While everyone else rushed outside, I darted into the guy's office, snatched his Omniplus Ultra off the desk, and sank down behind the furniture in the knee well, out of sight.

With trembling hands I sought to shuffle aside the protective wings of the device, utilizing all the instructions I had lovingly memorized, and expose its intimate control and display surfaces to my wanton gaze and lewd touch.

But I was doing something wrong! The expected blossoming failed to happen.

Instead, after some fumbling, the unit split open like a simple styrofoam clamshell container full of leftovers.

The interior gaped utterly vacant, except for a simple piece of printed cardboard.

Dumbfounded, I removed the cardboard and read the message.

Dear Consumer: the Omniplus Ultra is not what you need. You are already everything you thought it could do. Pass this message on as widely as you see fit. Or not. Hopefully yours, Pine Martin and Sheeda Waxwing, for the OmninfoPotent Corporation.

I put the card back inside, resealed the Omniplus Ultra, dropped it with a dull thud on the desk, and joined all my peers outside, waiting to resume our lives.

Author's Note

Paul Di Filippo has sold over 200 short stories and several novels in his career of three decades. His latest story collection, *A Palazzo in the Stars*, appeared from Wildside in 2015. He reviews for several venues, including *The Barnes & Noble Review*, *Locus Online*, and *Asimov's Science Fiction Magazine*. He likes to imagine that he is at the midpoint of his career, despite all actuarial statistics.

Virtually Correct

Marianne Dyson

Chief of Security Unlimited, Maxwell Bishop, slammed a meaty white fist onto his desk. "You're telling me that the government won't let me use holograms of real criminals committing real crimes to create virtual reality simulations?"

The thin black man from the Social Justice Department nodded his head. "That is essentially correct, Mr. Bishop."

Maxwell stood and leaned across his desk. "Do you realize how little time my guards might have to save you from one of those new beam weapons?" He shook his head and exhaled as he sat down heavily. "I *have* to use real crime scenes, or innocent folks won't have a chance."

"You misunderstand, Mr. Bishop," the man responded. "You may use crime scenes, but you must color-neutralize your characters. This removes unconscious bias from the virtual reality training experience, and helps people respond instead to suspicious actions not associated with race."

Maxwell had paid a fortune for his VR's, and any change was likely to ruin their effectiveness. There must be a way to get an exemption granted. He studied the man, noting how he sat nervously on the edge of his chair. He was probably a rehabbed offender drilled by the jail VR's to subconsciously defer to Maxwell's uniform.

"Mr. Crompton," Maxwell began, watching the man's response carefully.

"It's Compton, not Crompton," the man corrected.

Good, Maxwell thought, a stickler for details. He might be persuaded to let him use his VR's as a control. "Excuse me, Mr. Compton. Let's be perfectly honest here. I can no longer train my officers with actual scenes because most of them contain black suspects?"

"That is correct. In Houghton versus Crime Alert, it was determined that the use of virtual reality training using black criminal suspects resulted in the unnecessary shooting of Mr. Houghton by a Crime Alert security officer."

"Unnecessary my ass!" Maxwell shouted. "He had just grabbed a woman and obviously intended to rape her."

Compton cleared his throat. "Mr. Houghton slipped and grabbed her arm for support. The grand jury concluded there wasn't sufficient evidence to prove otherwise. His social rights were violated by Crime Alert's use of color-biased VR's."

Maxwell didn't believe that for a minute. Crime Alert's real mistake had been not training the officer to shoot to kill.

He leaned back and toyed with a small acrylic paperweight on his desk. It contained three different bullets, all of which he'd like to test on social rights lawyers. "Mr. Compton, do you admit statistics show blacks are much more likely to commit violent crimes than whites?"

The man shifted nervously in his seat. "What is your point?"

"My point is that I run a security outfit, not an arm of the Social Justice Department. I do not like the statistics, but I'd be a fool to ignore them. My VR's reflect the criminal profiles my officers are most likely to encounter. Using this data, I have earned the best record in Los Angeles for ridding the city of criminals who threaten innocent people, many of whom are black. I even hire young black men who might otherwise turn to crime to support themselves. Yet you say I am a racist."

"I never said you were a racist," Compton replied.

"But the government says if I use the VR's I use now—that I have found most effective in stopping crime, then I am promoting racial bias and therefore I am a racist."

"Some experts say using the data the way you do creates a self-fulfilling situation," Compton replied.

Maxwell frowned. This was getting nowhere. "How about if you let me continue using my VR's while the others color-neutralize, and see if I'm right?"

Compton shook his head. "Sorry, Mr. Bishop. My job is only to ensure that you color-neutralize your VR's to comply with the new social rights law." He reached into his breast pocket, and instinctively Maxwell drew his gun and leveled it at Compton's head.

The black man's eyes glowed white with fear. "What are you doing?" he squeaked.

"You're not from the Social Justice Department!" Maxwell boomed.

"Yes, yes, I am," the man pleaded. "I was getting some instruction disks from my pocket." He spread his hands wide, dropping a few small VR disks onto the desk. Maxwell lowered his gun, a bit embarrassed.

"Sorry, can't be too careful these days," Maxwell said. He wondered briefly if he would have reacted that way had the man been white. No, he was obviously responding to suspicious behavior. "Lots of criminals would like to shut my operation down, you know," Maxwell explained as he reholstered his gun.

Compton exhaled loudly and stood, surprising Maxwell by looking him in the eye. "Mr. Bishop, you will convert your characters to a neutral shade of green using the master set on these disks. Do you understand?"

Maxwell saw the man's fear had turned to anger now. Obviously his action had cost him a chance at an exemption. He sighed and took the disks. There was nothing to do but comply with the ridiculous law.

LOS ANGELES, CA—Our first encounter with alien life ended in tragedy today in a downtown Los Angeles neighborhood. The little green man died after being shot as it grabbed a black woman who was walking home. The security guard, a new employee of Security Unlimited, said he believed the alien was about to rape the woman, and shot it to protect her. Scientists believe the being was most likely having trouble adjusting to our gravity, and merely clutched the woman for support. The Department of Social Justice will be investigating the case to see if anything could be done to prevent future incidents.

Author's Note

Marianne Dyson is an award-winning children's author and a former NASA flight controller. For more information, visit www. MarianneDyson.com. About the story, she says just: "Racial profiling may have some unintended consequences."

Patent Infringement

Nancy Kress

Kegelman-Ballston Corporation is proud to announce the first public release of its new drug, Halitex, which cures Ulbarton's Flu completely after one ten-pill course of treatment. Ulbarton's Flu, as the public knows all too well, now afflicts upwards of thirty million Americans, with the number growing daily as the highly contagious flu spreads. Halitex "flu-proofs" the body by inserting genes tailored to confer immunity to this persistent and debilitating scourge, whose symptoms include coughing, muscle aches, and fatigue. Because the virus remains in the body even after symptoms disappear, Ulbarton's Flu can recur in a given patient at any time. Halitex renders each recurrence ineffectual.

The General Accounting Office estimates the Ulbarton's Flu, the virus of which was first identified by Dr. Timothy Ulbarton, has already cost four billion dollars this calendar year in medical costs and lost work time. Halitex, two years in development by Kegelman-Ballston, is expected to be in high demand throughout the nation.

NEW YORK POST
K-B ZAPS ULBARTON'S FLU
NEW DRUG DOES U'S FLU 4 U

JONATHAN MEESE
538 PLEASANT LANE
ASPEN HILL, MD 20906
Dear Mr. Kegelman and Mr. Ballston,

I read in the newspaper that your company, Kegelman-Ballston, has recently released a drug, Halitex, that provides immunity against Ulbarton's Flu by gene therapy. I believe that the genes used in developing this drug are mine. Two years ago, on May 5, I visited my GP to explain that I had been exposed to Ulbarton's Flu a lot (the entire accounting department of the Pet Supply Catalogue Store, where I work, developed the flu. Also my wife, three children, and mother-in-law. Plus, I believe my dog had it, although the vet disputes this.) However, despite all this exposure, I did not develop Ulbarton's.

My GP directed me to your research facility along I-270, saying he "thought he heard they were trying to develop a med." I went there, and samples of my blood and bodily tissues were taken. The researcher said I would hear from you if the samples were ever used for anything, but I never did. Will you please check your records to verify my participation in this new medicine, and tell me what share of the profits are due me.

Thank you for your consideration.

Sincerely,

> *Jon Meese*
> Jonathan J. Meese

FROM THE DESK OF ROBERT BALLSTON
KEGELMAN-BALLSTON CORPORATION
TO: MARTIN BLAKE, LEGAL
RE: ATTACHED LETTER
Marty—
Is he a nut? Is this a problem?
> Bob

INTERNAL MEMO, KEGELMAN-BALLSTON
TO: ROBERT BALLSTON
FROM: MARTIN BLAKE
RE: GENE-LINE CLAIMANT JONATHAN J. MEESE
Bob—
I checked with Records over in Research and, yes, unfortunately this guy donated the tissue samples from which the gene line was developed that led to Halitex. Even more unfortunately, Meese's visit occurred just before we instituted the comprehensive waiver for all donors. However, I don't think Meese has any legal grounds here. Court precedents have upheld the corporate right to patent genes used in drug development. Also, the guy doesn't sound very sophisticated (his *dog*?) He doesn't even know

that Kegelman's been dead for ten years. Apparently Meese has not yet employed a lawyer. I can make a small nuisance settlement if you like, but I'd rather avoid setting a corporate precedent for these people. I'd rather send him a stiff letter that will scare the bejesus out of the greedy little twerp.

Please advise.

    Marty

FROM THE DESK OF ROBERT BALLSTON
KEGELMAN-BALLSTON CORPORATION
TO: MARTIN BLAKE, LEGAL
RE: J. MEESE
Do it.

    Bob

MARTIN BLAKE, ATTORNEY-AT-LAW
CHIEF LEGAL COUNSEL, KEGELMAN-BALLSTON CORPORATION
Dear Mr. Meese,

Your letter regarding the patented Kegelman-Ballston drug Halitex has been referred to me. Please be advised that you have no legal rights in Halitex; see attached list of case precedents. If you persist in any such claims, Kegelman-Ballston will consider it harassment and take appropriate steps, including possible prosecution.

Sincerely,

    Martin Blake
    Martin Blake

JONATHAN MEESE
538 PLEASANT LANE
ASPEN HILL, MD 20906
Dear Mr. Blake,

But they're my genes!!! This can't be right. I'm consulting a lawyer, and you can expect to hear from her shortly.

    Jon Meese
    Jonathan J. Meese

CATHERINE OWEN, ATTORNEY-AT-LAW

Dear Mr. Blake,

I now represent Jonathan J. Meese in his concern that Kegelman-Ballston has developed a pharmaceutical, Halitex, based on gene therapy which uses Mr. Meese's genes as its basis. We feel it only reasonable that this drug, which will earn Kegelman-Ballston millions if not billions of dollars, acknowledge financially Mr. Meese's considerable contribution. We are therefore willing to consider a settlement, and are available to discuss this with you at your earliest convenience.

Sincerely,

Catherine Owen

Catherine Owen, Attorney

FROM THE DESK OF ROBERT BALLSTON
KEGELMAN-BALLSTON CORPORATION
TO: MARTIN BLAKE, LEGAL
RE: J. MEESE

Marty—

Damn it, if there's one thing that really chews my balls, it's this sort of undercover sabotage by the second-rate. I played golf with Sam Fortescue on Saturday, and he opened my eyes (you remember Sam; he's at the agency we're using to benchmark our competition). Sam speculates that this Meese bastard is really being used by Irwin-Lacey to set us up. You know that bastard Carl Irwin has had his own Ulbarton's drug in development, and he's sore as hell because we beat him to market. Ten to one he's paying off this Meese patsy.

We can't allow it. Don't settle. Let him sue.

Bob

INTERNAL MEMO, KEGELMAN-BALLSTON
TO: ROBERT BALLSTON
FROM: MARTIN BLAKE
RE: GENE-LINE CLAIMANT JONATHAN J. MEESE

Bob—

I've got a better idea. *We* sue *him*, on the grounds he's walking around with our patented genetic immunity to Ulbarton's. No one except consumers of Halitex have this immunity, so Meese must have acquired it illegally, possibly on the black market. We gain several advantages with this suit: We eliminate Meese's complaint, we send a clear message to other rivals who may be attempting patent infringement, and we gain a publicity circus to both publicize Halitex (not that it needs it) and, more importantly, make the public aware of the dangers of black market substitutes for Halitex, such as Meese obtained.

Incidentally, I checked again with Records over at Research. They have no documentation of any visit from a Jonathan J. Meese on any date whatsoever.

Marty

FROM THE DESK OF ROBERT BALLSTON
KEGELMAN-BALLSTON CORPORATION
TO: MARTIN BLAKE, LEGAL
RE: J. MEESE
Marty—
Brilliant! Do it. Can we get a sympathetic judge? One who understands business? Maybe O'Connor can help.

Bob

NEW YORK TIMES
HALITEX BLACK MARKET CASE TO BEGIN TODAY

This morning the circuit court of Manhattan County is scheduled to begin hearing the case of *Kegelman-Ballston v. Meese*. This case, heavily publicized during recent months, is expected to set important precedents in the controversial areas of gene patents and patent infringement on biological properties. Protestors from the group FOR US: CANCEL KIDNAPPED ULBARTON PATENTS, which is often referred to by its initials, have been in place on the court steps since last night. The case is being heard by Judge Latham P. Farmingham III, a Republican who is widely perceived as sympathetic to the concerns of big business.

This case began when Jonathan J. Meese, an accountant with the Pet Supply Catalogue Store...

CATHERINE OWEN, ATTORNEY-AT-LAW

Dear Mr. Blake,

Just a reminder that Jon Meese and I are still open to a settlement.

Sincerely,

Catherine Owen

MARTIN BLAKE, ATTORNEY-AT-LAW

CHIEF LEGAL COUNSEL, KEGELMAN-BALLSTON CORPORATION

Cathy—

Don't they teach you at that law school you went to (I never can remember the name) that you don't settle when you're sure to win?

You're a nice girl; better luck next time.

Martin Blake

NEW YORK TIMES

MEESE CONVICTED

PLAINTIFF GUILTY OF "HARBORING" DISEASE-FIGHTING GENES
WITHOUT COMPENSATING DEVELOPER KEGELMAN-BALLSTON

FROM THE DESK OF ROBERT BALLSTON

KEGELMAN-BALLSTON CORPORATION

TO: MARTIN BLAKE, LEGAL

RE: KEGELMAN-BALLSTON V. MEESE

Marty—

I always said you were a genius! My God, the free publicity we got out of this thing, not to mention the future edge—How about a victory celebration this weekend? Are you and Elaine free to fly to Aruba on the Lear, Friday night?

Bob

NEW YORK TIMES

BLUE GENES FOR DRUG THIEF

JONATHAN J. MEESE SENTENCED TO SIX MONTHS FOR PATENT
INFRINGEMENT

FROM THE DESK OF ROBERT BALLSTON
KEGELMAN-BALLSTON CORPORATION
TO: MARTIN BLAKE, LEGAL
RE: HALITEX

Marty, I just had a brilliant idea I want to run by you. We got Meese, but now that he's at Ossining, the publicity has died down. Well, my daughter read this squib the other day in some science magazine, how the Ulbarton's virus has in it some of the genes that Research combined with Meese's to create Halitex. I didn't understand all the egghead science, but apparently Halitex uses some of the flu genes to build its immune properties. And we own the patent on Halitex. As I see it, that means that Dr. Ulbarton was working with **OUR** genes when he identified Ulbarton's flu and published his work. Now, if we could go after *Ulbarton* in court, the publicity would be tremendous, as well as strengthening our proprietorship position.

But the publicity, Marty! The publicity!

Author's Note

Nancy Kress is the author of thirty-three books, including twenty-six novels, four collections of short stories, and three books on writing. Her work has won six Nebulas, two Hugos, a Sturgeon, and the John W. Campbell Memorial Award. Her most recent work is *Tomorrow's Kin* (Tor, 2017), the first novel of a trilogy based on her Nebula-winning novella "Yesterday's Kin" and extending its universe for several generations. Kress often writes about genetic engineering; "Patent Infringement" is a light-hearted look at a deadly serious subject.

Purgatory

Don Sakers

I don't *think* I'm in Hell. The last time I checked, Satan's teleport code was unlisted. But you can never be sure about these things. Science is always making improvements, and for all I know International TelePortal signed a contract with the Vatican last week.

So maybe this *is* Hell. Or more likely it's Purgatory, where Auntie Dora was always sure I would wind up anyhow.

What else would you call it? It isn't exactly the dark, featureless limbo she promised. Dark is what you see when you close your eyes, and as near as I can tell I don't even have eyes. Or anything else, for that matter. Oh, well, she got the "featureless" part right.

There's me, at least. I can think. It takes an effort, like forcing yourself to stay awake in a warm room in the wee hours of your second all-nighter in a row. Much easier to say goodbye to thought and just drift. A lot like watching threevee.

Sorry about that. I faded for a while. Where was I? Right, I don't *think* I'm in Hell. The last time I checked, Satan's teleport code was unlisted....

No, no, no! That's how this place is, even when you force yourself to think, you keep coming back to the same place. Now I know how a DVD feels.

Back to the same place. And how did I get here?

Simple. I punched a code, then stepped through the public TelePortal at First Avenue and Thirty-Fifth Street. I was one step behind my partner, Cufflink Lenny. He's called Cufflink because that's the sort of loot he likes to acquire—every middleclass mark has a drawer of cufflinks, tie-tacks, and tacky jeweled money-clips that he looks at once or twice a year. Any fence will give you good cash money for that stuff, and by the time the mark misses it, it's far too late.

Cufflink taught me almost everything I know about the business— retrieving teleport codes of solid upper-middleclass marks, where to find the best loot, wiping out your traces, dealing with the cops. All I added was my hacker's skill at breaking security codes.

Look at it from the mark's standpoint. You're rich enough to have your own TelePortal, instead of having to stand in line at the public station. Naturally you want the Portal in your house where you can show it off—but you don't want to give people like Cufflink and me access to your house.

So you put in a security feature. Give keys and codes to your closest friends. Anybody who doesn't have the key and know the code gets bounced to the public Portal nearest your house. Fundamentalists, bill collectors, and petty thieves are out of luck.

Cufflink and I aren't petty.

We made out okay. We chose our marks with care, and I wrote a worm that watched each account and notified us when the whole family had 'ported out for the weekend. We live well, Cufflink and me, middleclass at least but without any hassle since we always deal in cash. Three successful jobs a week, and the rest of the time we live in luxury.

Or we did, until now.

I stepped through the TelePortal, and the next thing I remember is... nothingness.

Damn it, TelePortals aren't supposed to go wonky.

And what happened to Cufflink? Did he do the job, or was he in his own little piece of Purgatory?

I'm right here with you, Bobby boy.

Cufflink?

I'm here.

I don't *hear* Cufflink—how can you hear without ears? His words are simply here, the way the words of a neon sign hang in front of you. Perhaps they've been here all along, and I haven't noticed until now.

Cuff, where the hell are we?

Don't you know?

I have my suspicions. I don't suppose you ever met my Auntie Dora?

What?

Never mind. The TelePortal malfunctioned, that's clear. And now we're stranded alone in...

Alone?

That voice isn't Cufflink's. I don't know how I can tell; you might as well say that it sounds different, although there's no such thing as sound in Purgatory. Call it taste, call it smell—whatever it is, I know that Cufflink and I aren't the only ones here.

Who's that?

Mary the Mouse, Bobby. Don't you remember me?

Sure I remember her. Mary the Mouse is one of our chief competitors. Half a dozen times in the last year, we've gone on a job only to find the mark completely cleaned out. Nothing you could prove in court—of course not—but each time the grapevine said Mary had beaten us to the punch. We'd talked with her, off and on over the years, about combining our talents. Mary was never interested. The Mouse, she says, is a solitary animal.

Fancy meeting you here, Mary, I think toward her.

Uppermiddle mark family on vacation for two months? comes her answer. *Do you think the Mouse would let an opportunity like that slip away?*

So you were after the same marks we were?

I can almost feel her shake her head. *Poor Bobby. You still don't understand, do you?*

I feel like a schoolkid when everyone else gets the joke.

Cufflink says, *You don't suppose they'll be back early, do you?*

Mary gives a mouselike squeal of a snort. *Not bloody likely, friend. These marks have been saving for two years for this trip.*

What if they never come back? What if they're in a crash, or they like it so much they decide to stay?

Then we're in deep trouble, Cuffy.

Who? What?

Cufflink ignores me. *Do you think any others will show up?*

We're here… do you suppose Tank and the Butcher won't be along soon? And Lady Godiva?

If I had a head, I would shake it. *What are you two talking about? Tank and the Butcher are from Jersey, Lady Godiva's in Texas… they won't use the same defective Portal we did.*

There is almost a sense of compassion in Cufflink's answer. *Bobby Boy, we'd better talk.*

But there isn't time, because suddenly a change comes over the world. Everything has been motionless, unchanging—now that's over, and for an instant all Purgatory seems to be shifting, sliding, moving off in a strange direction and carrying us with it.…

Mary the Mouse nods. *That'll be Tank coming in. The Butcher will be a few seconds behind him.*

What do you mean—? I start to ask, then the nonexistent air is filled with the bitter stench of teleportation, and a great voice fills our world. The voice of the uppermiddle homeowner who left his house empty for two months. Empty, but not untended.

Damn it, International TelePortal could at least have warned us before introducing a new service....

The deafening, inescapable voice chants on: "YOU HAVE REACHED THE KADOWSKI FAMILY. WE'RE NOT IN NOW, BUT AT THE SOUND OF THE BEEP, YOUR TELEPORT PATTERN WILL BE RECORDED AND STORED UNTIL WE RETURN...."

Author's Note

Don Sakers is a science fiction writer and librarian dedicated to diversity and frequently seen at science fiction conventions. He is the current book columnist for *Analog Science Fiction and Fact* magazine.

Delivery

Bud Sparhawk

"Something's wrong," I complained over the phone to the number on the packing slip. "I didn't order eight rolls of toilet paper."

The box had been delivered an hour earlier, somewhat larger than expected because of the extra tissue among the other items I'd ordered. I was certain that had not been one of the items I'd keyed in.

"I apologize, sir. It might be a mix-up because of the new ordering system. I will take the charge off of your account."

"Should I send them back or…"

"No need to do that. I'll just mark it off and thank you for your call."

The morning news was filled with politicians screaming at one another over a dozen different international disputes. It seemed that the amity of recent years was fast dissolving as the economy tumbled. I sighed. This had happened before and, as usual, would blow over within the year. I doubted it would affect me.

Elizabeth came home to have lunch with me. "Oh, I am so glad you remembered to order the toilet paper," she said when she saw the rolls on the counter. "We're nearly out, you know."

I debated admitting that I hadn't remembered and then thought better of it. "Someone needs to keep track," I said, and got a kiss in return. I promised myself that I'd call the store and have the charge put back on our account. It would be the honest thing to do.

"It's the new software we're running," the person at the other end of the line, said. "It runs some sort of algorithm against previous orders to see what you've been ordering. Not only does it improve our service to you, but it helps us fill orders more quickly and reduce our stocking costs."

"So that's why I got the toilet paper?" That feature would probably prove useful and keep me from missing things we needed—like the toilet paper. "I guess it will take care of my future grocery orders."

"More than that, sir," the cheerful agent replied. "The new software monitors all orders you've placed; books, clothing, recreational gear, and anything you might have bought on line. It uses that pattern to anticipate your needs and fulfill them."

"Uh, that could be embarrassing." I thought of a few purchases I'd rather Elizabeth didn't know about.

"The software is really good," the service agent went on rhapsodically—clearly a man enamored of his new toy. "The developers are continually improving it. Why, just yesterday they tied it into the weather system feed so we could prepare for snowstorms, floods, or even sunny weather when people might have swimwear needs."

"That might be useful," I said. "What next? Are they going to access the news channel feeds and predict the winner of the next election?"

"Analyzing the news is certainly something they're planning," he answered breezily. "Just part of our service improvement, sir."

I had to admit that the flow of goods into the house improved. Within a month I was getting half of the items on our grocery list without having to key them in. Within six months we received boxes with all our normal groceries without having to order at all.

Elizabeth was ecstatic over the thoughtful anniversary present she received and for which I didn't admit having forgotten, again. Somehow the magic provisioning software had analyzed my buying patterns, accessed our wedding date, and selected a piece of affordable jewelry that would please her.

I started to fall in love with the miraculous system that showered such bounty upon us.

Elizabeth was late getting home. "Everybody left early and clogged the roads," she said. "Some sort of political blow-up in Europe."

"I hope we can stay out of it this time," I answered. There was little hope for that. Given the way the global economy had evolved everybody got involved, willingly or not.

Elizabeth kicked off her shoes. "The bank was closed again today—third time this week. Something's up."

Other things followed as the software became ever more sophisticated. A pair of fur-lined gloves arrived just prior to the worst cold snap of the year. A set of replacement filters for the heat pump beat the warranty date by one day, and the bag of cat litter was right on time.

But it wasn't just purchases. We got regular reminders to fill the gas tank, pay the water bill, and even to tip the man who picked up the recycle bins.

It was wonderful. We were finally living in the bright future where all needs were satisfied with little effort on our part.

It started to feel like Christmas morning when the next present would be opened. I could hardly wait for the delivery truck to arrive to discover what the system anticipated, what needs that we were unaware of but would most certainly need within a very short time.

The only bad news was that the political posturing had become increasingly heated. Planes were in the air, ships at sea, and overhead the satellites watched.

A shipment arrived out of sequence, which might have been strange had it not been for the national unrest that seemed to be affecting everything. There were daily reports of riots in distant cities, a rising national crime rate, and some international sabre rattling. It seemed that little else was mentioned on the news channels.

The box was larger than usual for our weekly groceries and heavy: It took two burly men to carry it into the kitchen. I signed the sheet and waited until they were gone before I opened the box.

Inside were two backpacks, camping gear, hiking clothes, maps, a book on survival, two handguns, a rifle, and ten boxes of ammunition.

Author's Note

The era of internet-enabled shopping and intelligent systems is upon us, and it is merely a matter of time before this prophetic tale becomes all too possible. Like my short story "The Suit," this story might have already been overrun by events. In that case, you, yes, you sitting there, should consider what awaits you the next time the doorbell sounds.

Weaponized Ghosts of the 96th Infantry

James Van Pelt

"Until now, vengeful ghosts have been documented in history but never seen by science," said General Kilborne as he led the Secretary of Defense and Joint Chiefs of Staff into the forward bunker. "The army has known about them for years. We've studied the types of persons and the mindset that produces a violent, motivated spirit. Today you will see our first field test of the technology."

The Secretary of Defense, a large and solidly built man despite his age, looked out the two-inch thick blast windows that revealed a stretch of desert, bookended by a line of trees on the left and the city on the right. Between them, several hundred yards of heat-baked sand without a hint of cover shimmered in the sun. Bullets and mortars scarred the buildings. Broken windows stared blackly onto the waste. He glanced at the men filling the room, a serious, dour crowd. The war had dragged on for years against what the press had dubbed the "perpetual insurgency," an enemy that ambushed and booby-trapped and melted away in the face of superior force. Impossible to engage. Impossible to defeat.

Kilborne, in his startlingly clean uniform—medals and ribbons covering his chest—took a position at the view port. "Today we will demonstrate how we'll end this war."

An undersecretary, a young man, said, "I read the release. Do you expect us to believe that not only are ghosts real, but that the army can create them on demand, and that they will fight for us?"

The general nodded. "Yes, inspired by revenge, the oldest of human emotions, our weaponized ghosts hunt down their killers. No walls protect them. No weapons preserve them. Anyone who dares to take American soldiers' lives will face the tireless spirit of the dead."

The undersecretary thumbed through his papers. "Your information said that the soldiers were hand-picked for the training and medical preparations necessary for them to transition to, um…" he looked for a reference among his pages, "…post-corporeal status?"

"Our investigations into the technology show that some soldiers are stronger candidates. Men with families, for example, or ones who are newly engaged, are particularly good. If I would have had my way, the soldiers for this demonstration would be only the ones who recently learned they were to be fathers for the first time."

The Secretary of Defense said, "In other words, a man who has the most to live for is the best subject to become a vengeful spirit."

"Yes. If you'll look into the booklet the lieutenant gave you, you will find a picture and biography of the twenty American heroes who will be our pioneers to take us to peace."

"Brilliant," said the Secretary.

The undersecretary's mouth dropped open in surprise. "Wait, you plan to kill twenty soldiers right now, in front of us, as a proof of concept demonstration?"

The General checked his watch. "This is our Trinity, gentleman. You are about to witness a breakthrough in warfare as world-altering as the first nuclear detonation. Like the atomic bombs that brought Japan to its knees, I believe that our enemies, when they hear of what we do today, may very well put down their arms. What insurgent would fire at an American soldier if he knew that killing him would release an implacable vengeance? We will become their nightmares."

A plume of dust rose from beyond the trees to the left. Visible through the pall, a handful of humvees opened and spilled soldiers. The undersecretary checked the shell-damaged buildings to the right. They'd assumed an ominous watchfulness. He hadn't actually seen anything move, but he sensed weapons behind each dark opening.

The soldiers emerged from the behind the trees, spread in loose formation, guns carried in the ready position, walking across the sand.

The undersecretary, a tinge of horror in his voice, said, "How do you know they will be attacked here?"

The general said, "We leaked intel to the other side."

Now, the rest of the men crowded at the window. "It's about time we had a clear win," said one of them.

The soldiers drew farther and farther from their armored vehicles, heads high, alert, well trained.

"They don't know they are going to die," gasped the undersecretary.

"Of course not," said the general. "For them to make the jump to the post-corporeal, they have to be on a mission. The men believe they are beginning an assignment that will save the country. They are fighting for their future, for the things they love. We must provide them with sufficient motivation and rage to continue on in death."

The soldier nearest to a building stopped, dropped to his belly, gun pointed at a window. The other soldiers fell also. The bunker glass was too thick to hear their voices, but they were yelling. Several pounded at their weapons. None had fired.

Windows erupted in flame. Despite the insulation, the crackle of small arms penetrated. The soldiers writhed as bullets struck them. Several managed to get to their feet. They staggered toward the buildings, desperate fury on their faces, but they jerked and danced in a lead storm.

"This is where it gets interesting," said the general.

Finally, gunfire quit. Heads appeared in the windows, exulting in the carnage. No movement among the dead at first. Then, a smoke appeared to rise from the bodies, a black haze that eddied to head-height. There was no wind, but the blackness drifted toward the buildings, gained momentum, splashed against the walls like a dark wave, and flowed through the openings.

Suddenly, more gunfire. A man dove from a window, rolled on the sand, and then sprinted away. Smoke followed him, engulfed him, tore him to pieces.

A couple of the Defense Department men cheered, but the undersecretary wanted to turn away.

The general said, "What our enemy has just discovered is that you cannot stop the justice of the dead. You cannot negotiate or run. A ghost's vengeance has no limits. Our ghosts will root out their killers and destroy them."

Finally, the undersecretary closed his eyes. "You gave our men empty weapons?"

The general cleared his throat impatiently. "Of course. For the demonstration, they couldn't win the battle. They had to die. You must admit, it is a potent display of the technology."

The undersecretary looked onto the battlefield. Twenty soldiers lay crumpled in the desert. "You took everything from them."

A movement from the buildings caught the undersecretary's attention. Smoke poured from the windows and doors. It swirled, shifted about as if sniffing or searching.

"Those are our ghosts," said the general. "Our beautiful, deadly, vengeful ghosts."

The smoke paused in its uncertainty.

"Whose ghosts?" said the undersecretary.

Slowly at first, but then faster and with increasing purpose, the blackness rushed toward the bunker. The undersecretary wanted to speak, and he would have if the bunker's cement and thick glass had been any barrier at all. He opened his mouth, but in the end all he could do was scream.

Author's Note

James Van Pelt teaches high school English in western Colorado. Since 1990, his fiction has appeared in most of the major science fiction and fantasy magazines, and many anthologies, including several "year's best" collections. His latest novel, *Pandora's Gun*, came out in 2015.

TIME TRAVEL

If time travel ever becomes real, watch out! Modern habits can get you in trouble. Or you can make trouble, perhaps even for your past self. (Though you may not know what you've done.)

Operation Tesla

Jeff Hecht

An hour ago, Frankel had been on the holovision stage, being introduced as part of Team Beta. "It is 200 years since the birth of Nikola Tesla in 1856," the announcer had said. "Now Enigmas of the Twentieth Century is sending three teams of intrepid time travelers to find the legendary inventor's lost papers on wireless transmission, death rays, and energy before they went missing."

Now Frankel was back in Tesla's Manhattan, walking north on Sixth Avenue from 40th Street toward the entrance to Bryant Park. Massive yellow taxis zoomed by. A blue-uniformed policeman checked him out, then walked on past, but Frankel still worried. "I haven't heard from Watkins," he said to the phone transmitter buried in his collar.

He could hear Johnson's annoyance through his earbud receiver. "I told you dead spots are inevitable, even with the main transceiver in the Empire State Building. I know these phones are outdated for 2056, but they're hidden so nobody can see them. Everything you're wearing belongs in October 1937."

"Okay," Frankel agreed, reluctantly. He was grateful the rules let them use technology from any time in the twentieth century. It would have been hard to hide mobile phones built with vacuum tubes. Getting the colors of women's fashions would have been hard, but the three men on Team Beta could get by with drab dark suits, ties, and white shirts. Yet that hadn't helped all-male Team Alpha, who hadn't come back on time.

"Do you see Tesla yet?" Johnson's voice hissed through the earbud. "He should be near the public library, feeding the pigeons."

Inside the park, Frankel looked east toward the library. A tall, gaunt elderly man on a bench scattered crumbs to a flock of head-bobbing pigeons. Frankel recognized the inventor. He wondered what secrets of power beaming and wireless transmission were hidden in the missing papers. "I see him. Where's Watkins? I haven't heard from him in fifteen minutes."

"That's when he went into the Hotel New Yorker. I watched him from Cut Rate Drugs across Eighth Avenue; I'm having a soda inside. The hotel is a complex 43-story building, and something inside must be blocking his signal. I'll tell him you've spotted Tesla. If I can't reach him on his mobile, I'll head up to Tesla's room myself. I have a set of tools to get in."

"But what if I can't reach you?" Frankel worried. The operation depended on everyone keeping in touch so they could copy the papers and bring them to the retrieval point. They'd lose points if they had to be retrieved from different locations.

"Don't worry. You're perfectly safe. Nobody can eavesdrop on these calls. Just watch Tesla."

"Okay," Frankel agreed. Watching him was the easiest part of the operation. The goal of Operation Tesla was to bring back copies of Tesla's missing plans for death rays, power beams, and new communications devices. Enigmas of the Twentieth Century promised fame and a handsome reward for the team that came back with the best papers. Watkins and Johnson thought the papers were in the hotel room where he lived. The old fashioned mechanical locks should be easy to pick; the challenge was to find and copy the right papers.

Frankel settled down on a bench to keep a discreet eye on Tesla. The inventor was engrossed in his pigeons, as if he knew each one. Frankel opened a copy of the *New York Sun* he had bought from a newsdealer. The headlines ranged from world politics to sports. Roosevelt had talked on the transatlantic radio-telephone with the British Prime Minister about Adolf Hitler's meeting with Benito Mussolini. Police were questioning the staff of Bellevue Hospital about three lunatics who had vanished without trace from a locked ward. The Yankees had just beat the New York Giants four games to one in the World Series, and a sports writer wondered how long Lou Gehrig could keep playing.

Glancing at his authentic 1937 watch, Frankel saw it was time for another report. He scanned the park, and noted the inventor feeding the pigeons and three policemen walking down the path that went by him. "Tesla is still feeding the pigeons," Frankel said to his collar.

Nobody replied. That was odd. "Johnson! Watkins! Are you there?"

Worried that the police might have caught Watkins and Johnson trying to break into Tesla's hotel room, Frankel tried to look inconspicuous behind his paper. "Johnson, Watkins? Where are you? Rendezvous is in one hour and fifteen minutes!"

A heavy hand clamped down on Frankel's right shoulder, and as Frankel started to jump, a second clamped on his left. "All right, pal, we'll take you back to a nice, quiet padded cell," said one of the three policemen suddenly standing around him. They pulled away his newspaper and snapped handcuffs around his wrists, then patted him down, pulling out his wallet but not spotting the little transmitter sewn into his jacket.

"Johnson, Watkins, help!" He cried into his collar.

The first policeman shook his head. "If those are your pals from Bellevue, they're already at the precinct, talking to themselves just like you."

Frankel shivered. "They caught Team Alpha, and now they've got me," he said into his collar phone. "I don't know what tipped them off."

The policeman rolled his eyes.

Author's Note

Jeff Hecht makes his living writing about science and technology for *New Scientist* and other magazines, and writes books about lasers and fiber optics. His short science fiction is a sideline that has appeared in many magazines and anthologies. "Operation Tesla" originally appeared in *Nature*.

The Man Who Brought Down
The New York Times

Paul Levinson

He came down the stairs, brandishing a copy of *The New York Times*.
I don't think I'd ever seen my father so angry.

"Nothing!" He threw the paper on to the kitchen table. "Not a word
about my work!"

"Charles…" Mama stuck her head in from the dining room. "You
can't control what they print. There's nothing you can do—"

"Oh, there's something I can do all right," Papa said. "They promised
me. They promised they'd run the story this time. Bastards—"

Mama blushed.

Papa looked at me, standing by the door. "I'm sorry, Rebecca. I didn't
mean to curse like that."

"It's okay, Papa. I once heard a boy say that in the school yard." I
smiled my little-girl smile. I'd always be his little girl. "It's hard being an
inventor of something. My friend Janey once wrote a great poem—and it
was so good, no one believed she really wrote it."

Mama was next to him now, her arms around him, trying to soothe him.
"No one believes in people who invent things in their garages any more. It's
all big corporations now. No point beating your head against the wall."

"There's a point," Papa insisted. "What's the use of inventing
anything if no one knows about it?"

"You can't really blame the newspapers," Mama said. "If you don't
even have a patent, how can you expect the *Times* to—"

"Patent?" Papa yelped. "How am I supposed to go about getting a
patent on this machine? Just file a blueprint of my design with the Patent
Office? It's a *time machine*, for God's sake! If someone else built it, if it
fell into the wrong hands, it could wreak havoc on our world!"

"Okay then," Mama said. "How about some good hot oatmeal for
breakfast?" She gestured towards a simmering pot on the stove.

"Let's sit down and eat. Forget about the *Times*. There's nothing you can do about it."

"Yes, there is." Papa sat down, ready to eat, but not mollified, "They promised me they'd print the story this time. Now they're going to pay."

Whatever Papa did to make the newspaper pay, it didn't take him away from home very much.

Or maybe it did, and I didn't understand.

I overheard snippets of conversation, coming out of their bedroom late at night.

"You see, Dear, I could be gone for months, even years at a time, and you wouldn't notice the difference, because if I returned just a second after I left, it would seem to you and the world like I'd never been gone."

"Wouldn't you look older?" Mama asked.

"Well, I guess I would at that," Papa replied. "But do I?"

"No," Mama said.

"I guess that's because in fact I have not been gone for years or even months. I'm getting everything done in just a few hours, or maybe a day or two, each time. It's not that hard to trip them up on little things."

"I still don't like it," Mama said. "It's dangerous."

I can't recall the first time I noticed there that was a change in the world, because I guess it came on too gradually, like winter, sometimes. One day I just realized that things had become different—people were just more irritable, more jumpy, than they used to be. As if they couldn't trust in things the way they used to.

It was harder to tell with Papa, because he was tired and irritable anyway from all of his travelling.

He'd get up very early some mornings, fetch the paper from the front porch, and take it upstairs to his den. And he'd come down a little while later, a look of determination on his face as he kissed Mama and me goodbye and walked out the door to the garage. And then the door would open again, just a minute or two after, and Papa would come back in the house. Sometimes with rain or even snow on his face, though the morning was bright and sunny. He'd look at Mama and me, and not say a word to us, though I once heard him mumble to himself as he walked back upstairs. "I'll see what the paper looks like tomorrow."

This went on for years and years. Papa was able to keep his job at the Post Office because the whole routine never took much of his time—he was never late. He gradually seemed to become more satisfied. He never spoke again of his time machine, or *The New York Times*. He just carried that newspaper with him, up and down those stairs....

Eventually, I went away to college. Eventually, Papa retired from the Post Office. Eventually, he retired from his routine.

I have a husband and family of my own now. We live across the country. I come back every year with my husband and kids to visit Mama and Papa on the holidays.

I got a few minutes alone with Papa last December as he sat in his rocking chair on the front porch.

"It looks the same," he said, and pointed out to the lawn and beyond, "but somehow different."

"Well, it's a different world today, Papa. Not like it was when I was first growing up. Everyone's in a hurry today, rushing, pushing, shoving."

"Like they're afraid if they don't move quickly enough they'll make some terrible mistake," Papa said.

I looked at him.

"I guess it's my fault," he said.

"You can't know that for sure," I said.

"But I was right to do it!" He picked up a copy of *The New York Times* from underneath his chair. "They promised me they'd run the story. They promised!"

"I know, Papa."

"So, if they were going to lie to me, and the world, the least I could do was expose them for what they were. Maybe it undermined people's confidence in things, I don't know. But I had no choice. All the news that's fit to print? Hardly. All the omissions and errors that's fit to print—that's more like it! No wonder it's been dropping in circulation like a stone. No wonder all everyone's talking about these days is fake news. They say it's because of the Internet. But it's me."

He pointed to a little box on the bottom of the front page.

"They didn't believe in my time machine? Well, I had the last laugh. I picked a story, a fact in a story, a quote in a story, each time I went out. And I went back just a little bit in time in my machine and changed it—so the *Times* wound up having it wrong. I did it with other newspapers too—they're all the same. And it embarrassed them, got them so jittery, that now they make mistakes all the time without my help. It's become the norm!" He laughed, with a mixture of joy and something much darker. "They don't need me and my machine any more to make them look foolish."

His finger jabbed the bottom of the page. "*Errata*. Oh, they listed mistakes on their own, once in a while, before I got started. But now those apologies are here on the front page almost every day. That's my lasting gift to the newspapers of the world. No one will really have confidence in them ever again."

Author's Note

Paul Levinson, PhD, is Professor of Communication & Media Studies at Fordham University in New York City. His science fiction novels include T*he Silk Code* (winner of Locus Award for Best First Science Fiction Novel of 1999), *Borrowed Tides* (2001), *The Consciousness Plague* (2002), *The Pixel Eye* (2003), *The Plot to Save Socrates* (2006), *Unburning Alexandria* (2013), and *Chronica* (2014)—the last three of which are also known as the Sierra Waters trilogy, and are historical fiction as well as science fiction. His stories and novels have been nominated for Hugo, Nebula, Sturgeon, Edgar, Prometheus, and Audie Awards. His most recent nonfiction books are *McLuhan in an Age of Social Media* (2015), and *Fake News in Real Context* (2016). He co-edited *Touching the Face of the Cosmos: On the Intersection of Space Travel and Religion* in 2016. He appears on CNN, MSNBC, Fox News, the Discovery Channel, National Geographic, the History Channel, NPR, and numerous TV and radio programs. His 1972 LP, *Twice upon a Rhyme*, was re-issued in 2010. He was President of the Science Fiction and Fantasy Writers of America, 1998-2001. He reviews television in his InfiniteRegress.tv blog, and was listed in *The Chronicle of Higher Education*'s "Top 10 Academic Twitterers" in 2009.

The Thunder of Sound

H. Paul Shuch

By the time I got home, I was totally wiped. Not that I don't find every trip exhausting, what with all the precautions you have to take nowadays. After all, as every time traveler knows, anything you change in the future, even the tiniest little detail, ripples back through the spacetime continuum, all the way back to the present, sometimes with disastrous results. So, naturally, the Temporal Security Administration brain-scans you coming and going.

Of course, I know the rules. I've done this a zillion times. But this trip was especially stressful, probably because of that close call I had next month. It took every bit of willpower I could muster to keep myself from swatting that mosquito. I mean, you're fighting against ten thousand years of evolution and instinct there, and to sit idly by and watch that little bastard suck my blood was far more painful than the modest pinprick of contact.

Damn, how I wanted to kill that thing!

But, I didn't. I know enough to adhere strictly to the motto of the Bradbury Society: take nothing but pictures, leave nary a footprint. So I just clenched my jaw, held my breath, and hoped against hope that nourishing a single insect wasn't going to bring about the End of the World as We Know It. Sometimes, no matter what you dream up in REM sleep, it's the wrong move.

I lucked out that time, and for the briefest moment, even considered giving up my wandering ways altogether. But time travel is addictive, as exhilarating as it is exhausting. There's not one of us who can give it up for good, no matter what we say during a share at the TA meetings. So, here I was again, a month earlier, getting back from yet another trip.

Did I mention that I was even more cautious than usual this time? Even checked my boots for butterflies before launching homeward. By the times I got back, I was a nervous wreck.

I shouldn't have worried. Everything was the same as when I left. I made sure of that. I checked the answering machine; same played messages. Booted the computer; same MicroHard Windoze logo. Launched an app; same Green Screen of Death. Picked up my Samsung Universe 7 dumbphone to feel the reassuring warmth of its battery. Flipped on the radio; same Serious MX satellite channels. Shouted "Alexa, fuck off!" to no one in particular, and that familiar deep, masculine voice responded with the usual: "I'm sorry, I don't know the question to the answer I just heard."

Yes, everything appeared perfectly normal. So, I opened up the Humidaire, grabbed myself the usual nice, warm beer, asked Serious for Channel 760, and tilted back in the LazyGirl to listen to some music.

Instant relaxation. Boy, how I love those Haydn Variations on a Theme by Brahms!

Author's Note

H. Paul Shuch, a retired professor of physics and engineering, travels unidirectionally through time at a rate of 23 hours 56 minutes 4.1 seconds per sidereal day. He has thus far been unsuccessful in returning to the starting point, leaving still untested his hypothesis that changes in the future ripple backward through the time-space continuum, modifying the past. He would have written a longer story for this anthology, but he just didn't have the time.

In the Speed of Time

Douglas Van Belle

I slowly raised my hands and considered my options. I didn't really have any. Late on a Friday evening, the nearest person who might conceivably come to my rescue was a dozen floors away, which the man with the gun would know if he really was me.

If he really was me. I knew it was a ludicrous thing to even imagine, but I was having trouble dismissing the idea. He looked a little heavy and haggard, but there was no mistaking the face from my mirror.

"Time travel." He answered the unasked question.

Those two simple words were the perfect thing to say. They cut straight through the melee in my head and gave me an answer to the obvious question without actually telling me much. He was trying to define the logic I would use to engage the situation, but still keep me in the dark. It was exactly what I would have done.

"I presume you aren't dropping by to deliver stock tips and lotto numbers."

He shook his head, apologetic. The movement was little more than a spastic twitch.

"So... what is this then?" I stepped over and poured two tumblers full of Scotch. We both needed to settle our nerves. The hand holding the gun was trembling. "Some kind of super geeky way to commit suicide?"

"Maybe in an abstract philosophical sense," he said. "But killing you won't really be suicide in any meaningful way."

He gestured with the gun as I brought his drink over. It was an odd wave of the weapon, but it was clear he meant for me to keep my distance.

"So the paradox thing isn't an issue?" I set the tumbler full of scotch it on the coffee table in front of him and stepped back.

"No." He waited until I took a second step back before he picked up his drink and pointed the gun just a little off to the side. "It would take weeks to get you up to speed on the theory, but the gist is that different moments in time move forward at the same rate. So it will take three years for the effects of this to reach the day I left, and by then, the moment in time that I'm from will be three years farther into the future."

"So it's like two different cars on the same train." I said, trying to keep it conversational, trying to ease him into revealing more.

"Nice analogy," he said it like he was impressed.

"It wasn't the first thing that popped into your head when it was explained to you?" I asked, surprised.

He shook his head.

"And if you're surprised by it, that also means that you didn't experience my side of this, did you?"

He shook his head again.

"Fascinating," I muttered.

"It's more fascinating than you can imagine." He finally took a sip of the scotch, but it was a very small sip. "Even if the machine hadn't worked, the theory behind it offers such an elegantly simple explanation for all the big puzzles of cosmology that it would have been worth the buttload of money I threw at it. Dark matter is actually gravitational pull from the past, tugging the matter in the present moment back toward the middle of galaxies and pulling galaxies back toward the Big Bang. Dark energy is the gravity of the future, pulling the universe toward a near infinite diffusion. Inflation occurred because at the moment of creation there was no past, so the pull of the future was infinite. There are no bubble universes and no multiverses because inflation stopped the quantum instant there was enough time in the past to pull the rate of expansion below lightspeed. Add functions representing the density of the mass in the past and the future, and how gravitational pull across time decreases as those moments become more distant in time, and you can explain the changing rate of expansion of the universe. We know that the universe and time are finite because expansion stopped, and so on."

He seemed relieved to have something to talk about. That was good. If killing me was a need rather than a desire, it might give me something to work with.

"And time travel itself?" I asked. "How does that work?"

"I know what you're doing," he said, giving me a sad but wry smile before indulging me with a bit more information. "Entanglement and non-locality can be recast in terms of quantum moments in time. Time travel is then made possible by the mechanism that allows gravity in the past and the future to pull on the now. Unfortunately, the math on that looks like something barfed up by Schrödinger's ill-tempered dog. I... we can't even come close to sorting it out."

"That must be some math, if we can't understand it," I said.

He nodded.

"So, if there are no paradoxes, and you can't kill yourself before you become the super villain that destroys the universe, then why are you here?"

That pushed him in the wrong direction. I saw it the moment I said it.

"There are other reasons for me to kill you." He pointed the gun at my face and took a deep breath like he was steeling his nerve.

The tremble was back in his hand. He clenched his jaw and lowered the shaking gun to point it at my chest. The trembling grew worse, and he had to set down his drink and use both hands to try to hold the gun steady. He focused everything he had on his aim, and I could see him silently mouthing the count down: "Three, two, one."

He hit zero, and nothing happened. A very long second later, he lowered the gun, grabbed his drink, and took a big, slow sip of the scotch. He looked desperate.

"It's okay, Paul, you aren't a murderer," I said, soothing.

"Yes, I am." The way he said it left no doubt.

"Jesus," I muttered. "I know that I'm an aggressive, always-play-to-win asshole, but I can't imagine even contemplating murdering someone."

"I stumbled into it, to be honest." He took another long slow, sip of the Scotch. "When meddling in the past didn't fix anything, the science team decided that history just snapped back into place the instant we were recalled to the present. Their best theory was that we were just projecting a bubble of the 'now' moment into a reflection of the past. Time travel was an illusion, and I had basically built a huge, fully tactile, twenty billion dollar historical video game. Interesting for historical research, but not much else. It took a few months before they figured out they were wrong, very wrong. The things we did in the past were real, they could just never change our present."

"And in those few months when you thought it was just a game, you went back in time and killed someone."

"Hitler," he said.

"Oh, for Christ's sake," I huffed. "What turned me into such a god-damned drama queen? I know for a fact that I could never for a single second think that killing that evil bastard was murder."

"True," he admitted. "If he was the only one I killed, I don't think it would bother me at all, but I wasn't always tidy about how I took him out."

"You weren't always tidy about it?" I scowled. "How many times did you kill him?"

"I don't know." He shrugged. "A lot."

"Why?" I was puzzled. "I can imagine doing it once or twice, but over and over to the point that I'd lose track of how many times I'd done it, really doesn't sound like me."

"I guess you could say it was cathartic," he said. "Killing someone who deserved to die could never make up for the unfairness of losing her, but it helped." Tears started welling in his eyes, and he took a big gulp of his scotch. "Living without her is unbearable, and putting a bullet through Hitler's head was about the only thing that kept me from putting one through mine."

"Without her?" It took me several seconds to put the pieces together. "You mean without Beth?"

"It was a freak accident." He started to take another sip, realized that he was doing exactly what I had hoped he might do when I gave him the full tumbler of scotch, and he set the glass down. "I think that made it worse, not being able to blame anyone."

"That's what you wanted to fix," I whispered, more to myself than to him. "That's why you threw money at an insane scheme to build a time machine."

"You can't believe that you're capable of caring that much about her, can you?" Tears were rolling down his cheeks. There was no doubt that the man truly was devastated. "You can't imagine you love her so deeply that losing her would drive you to suicide, but you do, and it damn near did. A little over three years ago, on this very night, on this very couch, I put this gun in my mouth and tried my damnedest to pull the trigger."

"Tonight? Beth dies tonight?"

"Yes… no… The accident was actually in the early afternoon." He choked up as he said it, a wheezing gasping breath. It rattled him, but he pushed on. "The cops spent most of the day trying to get a hold of me before she died. But we could be incredibly difficult to contact, especially when we let everyone in the office start the holiday weekend a day early. For a rich bastard, we are surprisingly kind."

He wiped the tears away with his sleeve and re-aimed the gun. His hand was still trembling, but it was far steadier than it had been a few moments earlier

"No, don't." I pleaded. "Just looking at you, I can see how much you've suffered, and I know you must think you're doing me a favor by coming back to pull that trigger for me, but please, no. No matter how horrible it's going to be, I don't want you to kill me to save me from the pain of living without her."

"I'm not here for you." He looked confused, and then he abruptly started laughing. It sounded maniacal. "I came here to get Beth back."

"You know that doesn't make any sense." I tried my best to speak calmly and clearly. "When you go back, the changes you make here will never catch up to you. That's why you couldn't save Beth."

"I already saved her," he said. "I called her and kept her on the phone long enough to delay her coffee run. That was all it took. She still stumbled and sprained her ankle, which is curious, but when she fell into the street there was no bus there to hit her."

"And when you go back…"

"I'm not going back. You are. Or at least, your corpse is." The gun was dead steady and pointed at my face. He had found his resolve.

I shook my head and held out my hands, pleading silently. I knew I should understand it, but it just refused to settle in my head.

"There is no front car on the train," he said. "There is no single privileged instant of now where the undetermined possibilities of the future slip into the certainty of history. This moment is just as real as any of the others, and now that I have saved Beth, I am going to take it from you. I am going to live in this moment, with her, for the rest of my life."

"Fine, I agree!" I shouted.

It was too late to stop that shot, but he reacted to my shout just enough to push the shot to the left. It felt like a firecracker going off against my cheek, and I could feel the blood dribbling down the edge of my jaw.

"What do you mean, you agree?" He was confused.

"You can have this moment," I said. "I'll go back to yours."

"Where there's a time machine just sitting there, locked on to this moment, and waiting to whisk you back here to undo this," He said.

"I won't," I said. "I swear."

"I'd like to believe you. I really would, but if you're alive, you will," he said. "You won't be able to bear living without her."

"Leaving her behind with you is different than losing her like you did," I said. "I will be miserable without her. I know that, but I'll also know that she'll be alive, and she'll be with a version of me who will keep her happy for the rest of her life. It's not what I want, but I choose that over dying. You'd choose that over dying any day."

"I can't risk it," he said.

"If you let me go, you don't have to live with the guilt of killing me," I said. "Think about those people who died from you going back to kill Hitler. That wasn't really your fault, but this… If you kill me in cold blood, the guilt will eat you alive, and you know it."

Tears streamed down his face as he tossed me a small electronic device. It had to be the recall unit. It was about the size of a deck of cards and it looked like an antique cigarette case, but when I opened it I found a thumb scanner and a button hidden under a small guard. It was exactly as I would have designed it.

I heard the gun hit the floor, heavy, solid. He was sobbing, overcome and helpless. All I had to do was grab the gun. I could end it with a bullet. I could stay right there, in that moment, with Beth. That would certainly be a hell of a lot better than jumping into a future where she'd been dead three years.

I put my thumb on the scanner and pushed the button.

Author's Note

Douglas A. Van Belle is a Senior Lecturer in Media Studies at Victoria University of Wellington. In addition to being a screenwriter and novelist, he has published extensively in politics, media, and policy. His fourth novel, *The Kahutahuta* (2017) is his first work for young readers, joining *Barking Death Squirrels* (2011), *The Care and Feeding of Your Lunatic Mage* (2011), and 2016's science fiction thriller, *Breathe. Breathe* will also hit the screens in a few years, as will forthcoming novels, *The List* (2018) and *A World Adrift* (2019).

Cease and Desist

Jay Werkheiser

Davey sighed and paused his TV show. The doorbell rang again, somehow sounding more insistent. He sighed again, peeled himself from the couch, and brushed potato chip crumbs from his shirt.

He opened the door a crack. "What is it?"

A man stood on his porch, looking as stiff as his suit collar. "I'm here to serve you with a Cease and Desist letter from my client, Mr. David Keeler."

"I'm David Keeler."

"Right. The letter is from the future you. Didn't you read about the new time travel devices?"

"Saw it on TV. Wait, future me?"

"Can I come in, Mr. Keeler?"

"Davey." He sighed, and opened the door all the way.

The lawyer stepped in, glanced at the grease-covered couch, and continued to stand. "The letter states that your eating and, uh," glancing down at Davey's ample gut, "exercise habits are injuring my client, and that you are to cease immediately."

"Hey, I ain't hurting nobody but myself—"

"Exactly."

"Harrumph." Davey crossed his arms over his gut. "I can eat whatever I want."

The lawyer rifled through his attaché case. "My client already knew you wouldn't comply—"

"How'd he know that?"

Raised eyebrow.

"Right."

"So he filed a complaint in Federal court. Here's your summons."

Davey found a lawyer at the local mall. "Didn't your office used to be a shoe store?"

The lawyer, Thomas H. Cromwell, Esquire, squinted at him through glasses thicker than the chocolate bar in Davey's hand. "It might have been."

"Last month?"

"You want a lawyer or not?"

Davey eyed the guy's plaid suit. "I guess so."

"Who's suing you?"

Davey handed him the court papers.

Cromwell held the chocolate-stained papers up to his nose, squinted, and dropped them onto his desk. "I see. What are you planning to do about it?"

"Hire a lawyer."

"Right. Court date's coming up soon."

Davey glared at him. "What do you suggest? Can he, uh, I mean can I really force me, um, myself to eat healthy crap? And *exercise*?"

"That'll be up to the judge."

"Can you stop him?"

"We'll see, now won't we?"

Davey noticed that his eyes, magnified as they were by his glasses, held not even a microscopic glint of confidence.

The Honorable Linda Livingston presided over the case, which had become a bit of a media circus once Davey—Future Davey—had aired his complaint on the talk show circuit. Health zealots, individual rights activists, and just plain whackos dueled with chants and picket signs outside the courthouse. Davey slouched in his seat next to his lawyer, trying to be invisible.

"Your honor," Cromwell said, "I move to dismiss this case."

"On what grounds?"

"On the grounds that you have already ruled in my client's favor."

The judge frowned. "What makes you say that?"

"Because there have been no other suits from the future, which means that in the future you have already established precedent against such cases."

"Objection," Future Davey's lawyer said. "Courts in the future have ruled that no such case may be filed before this point in time so as not to interfere with this court's ruling."

"Motion denied." She turned her attention to Future Davey's lawyer. "You may present your case."

"The David Keeler of this time is causing direct harm to my client. Further, his habits violate the Healthy Eating Act of 2024 and the Fitness Act of—"

"Objection," Cromwell said. "Those laws haven't been enacted yet."

"But they have for my client."

The judge turned her steely gaze on Cromwell. "Well?"

"Erm… the actions weren't illegal when my client committed, um, is committing them. Ex post facto."

"Agreed." She turned her attention to Future Davey's lawyer.

"But surely it's unfair to expect my client to work with laws that are decades out of date. Ad ante facto."

"That's not a thing."

"Not yet."

"Counsel will only cite law that currently exists."

The lawyer grumbled. "Okay, perhaps Mr. Keeler's actions are legal—"

"They are."

"But they still harmed my client. Reckless endangerment."

"He's endangering no one but himself."

"Exactly. And that's who is suing him."

Cromwell sputtered.

Seeing his cushy life vanish before his eyes, Davey stood. "Your Honor, may I say something?"

The judge threw up her arms. "Why not?"

"I know my lifestyle is unhealthy." He patted his gut. "That I should eat better, and exercise more. But I put in long hours at the fast food place, and I'm tired at the end of my shift, so I just bring a bag home. Exercise? Sure, I tried it, but it takes too much commitment."

"That's just laziness," Future Davey's lawyer said.

"Exactly!" Davey replied. "And it seems I still will be lazy in the future." He pointed at his rotund future self. "He could have started eating right and exercising at any time. But it was easier to hop in a time machine and force me to do it for him. I'm not proud of it, but that's exactly who we are."

"Objection."

"Goes to the character of the plaintiff," Cromwell said.

"I'll allow it. Court is in recess while I make my decision."

Davey melted into his seat when the judge returned with her ruling.

"This case," she said, "is about responsibility. Both Mr. Keelers are lazy and irresponsible, to be sure, but I can only judge the present one. I rule in favor of the plaintiff." She smacked the bench with her gavel.

Davey turned to Cromwell in a panic. "You mean I can't eat fast food? I have to exercise?"

"Don't worry," Cromwell said. "I've prepared an appeal of sorts, just in case."

"Good! When do we file it?"

"About fifteen years ago."

"What?"

"That's when you graduated high school, right? Decided not to go to college, sat around watching TV, started working at the fast food place."

"Yeah, that's right."

"So why should you do all the work getting in shape? Let's make him do it."

"Yeah!" Davey beamed for a moment, then his smile fell. "Only..."

"What?"

"Who's he going to sue?"

Author's Note

The idea for this story came from a student who, during a two-hour biochemistry class, drank an entire 2-liter bottle of soda. When I questioned the wisdom of his choice, he shrugged and said, "Future me is going to hate me." That set my writer senses tingling, and on the drive home, the entire story clicked into place. Writing a story is often a grueling battle with characters, words, and plot, but this one practically wrote itself. For those worried about the student who inspired this story, I'm pleased to note that he is now graduated and making healthier choices.

SHAGGY DOGS

A venerable tradition in both science fiction and fantasy is the shaggy dog story, ending with a dreadful pun, or at least with a baddabum! punch line. There's at least one earlier in the book. Here we have soggy zombies, dinosaurs, and biomedical technology.

Return of the Zombie Sea Monster

Michael F. Flynn

I was sitting on the broad, wooden front porch, listening to the ocean breakers at dusk when I saw the gnarled, stooped, leathery, grizzled, salty old sea dog hobble across the beach. A cold hand of fear gripped my heart. That was way too many adjectives. That was when I knew. I was a character in a badly written story.

"Avast!" growled the man with the peg leg named Captain Bob. I didn't know what the rest of him was named, so I called him Bob, too. He wore a pea coat and clenched his teeth around a clay pipe. On his left shoulder perched a parrot and what I hoped was dandruff.

"Doesn't it bother you, being a cliché?" I asked him, as I invited him to a rocker on my left.

"Now, you watch your mouth there, matey," he snarled. "The c-word is demeaning."

Then Ilse came out to the porch. She was a long-legged, slinky, golden-haired, sun-tanned Swede. She had as many adjectives as Bob, but they were more interesting ones. "Vat is wrong, dahling?" she murmured in her sultry voice.

"Bob, here, was just about to give me an Ominous Warning."

"Which I'll be givin' ye, if ye close yer pie hole for a minute," growled the salty old sea dog. Then he leaned toward us and whispered harshly, "Sea monster."

Ilse looked about in sudden panic. "Vhere? I see nothing."

"Nay, ye fatuous love interest. This be a monster conjured from the vasty deep. He creeps ashore on dark and foggy nights—coincidentally, much like this one—and roams the beaches looking for brains to feast upon."

"Nothing but surfers out there," said Pam, the girl-next-door rocket scientist, who also joined us on the porch. "That's more like a snack than a feast."

I scratched my head. "I dunno. Sea monsters sound like fantasy, not hard science fiction. *Analog* might not go for it. Besides," I added, "as you know, Bob, we slew that monster last time."

"Arrh," growled the old man with the wooden leg, "that we did, matey. But it be a-coming back to life."

"You mean… a *zombie* sea monster?" I raised my eyes upward, off the page, and implored the Author, "Is that the best You can do? Aren't You pushing this zombie fad too far?"

"Whate'er ye do, matey," warned Captain Bob, "when the fog be a-rollin' in, 'tis death to venture out."

"Don't go," the parrot contributed to our symposium. "Don't go."

"Well," said Captain Bob, patting down his pockets, "I be running low on me pipe tobaccy, now; so I'll just mosey on over to the 7-11 and fetch me a pouch."

"Captain Bob!" I cried. "You mustn't go out in the fog! You're the colorful sidekick. That means you'll get eaten by the monster. Stay here safe behind the screen door of this seaside cottage, which the monster inexplicably is unable to break through. The only reason you're going out is that the Author is forcing you to go."

"Ah," scoffed Pam the rocket scientist. "The 'Author Hypothesis'."

"Yes, and he has a Plot and makes us act to fulfill it—just like he makes the reader turn the page at this point."

"Oh, come on," said the comely, brunette rocket scientist. "Everything that happens in this story can be explained by natural laws and our own motives and purposes. There is no scientific evidence for your Author anywhere in the story."

"Oh, yeah?" I retorted. "Then why do we speak in clichés? Why is the Plot so banal? *Why are we all stereotypes?* Look at us. The handsome action hero. The colorful sidekick, who will do something boneheaded simply because the Plot demands it. The sultry but vapid fiancé with whom I only think I am in love. The comely girl who is so smart she is a rocket scientist, whom I will see as my true soul-mate after Ilse's brains are eaten and she removes her glasses."

"So what am I," said the parrot. "Chopped liver?"

Yes, what was to be the parrot's fate? Suddenly, I was inspired by the Author. "After Bob is devoured, you will fly back here to the cottage, blood-spattered and alone, and that will symbolize Bob's gruesome death in a touching manner."

"I'm not sure any gruesome death can be in a touching manner," said Ilse.

"And why would I fly back here," the parrot demanded, "and not to my own cage on Bob's sloop, where my food is? Because it would make for a heart-breaking scene? Awwk! What a plot hole!"

"But, Lance," said Pam perkily, "everything can be explained scientifically. Captain Bob has early onset Alzheimer's, and that's why he'll forget his own warning. The Science of Psychology tells us that Ilse will only run once she realizes that she can never compete with a pert, girl-next-door rocket scientist for your favors. The sea monster evolved to feast off the surfers, vacationers, and other detritus; and it was reanimated by nuclear wastes seeping into the ocean from exploding power plants. See? It's all scientifical!"

Captain Bob gauged the thickness of the fog and checked his watch. "Well, best get this over with."

"I should start packing," said Ilse. "I can't run from a zombie sea monster without my make-up valise and my two suitcases of expensive and fashionable clothing. And my heels; I have to run across a sandy beach from a sea monster in high heels."

"Awwk!" said the parrot. "This might be worth it just to see a sea monster in high heels."

Pam stood. "And I'll put on my white lab coat—in which I look adorably pert and fetching—and, using recycled materials (conveniently available in this seaside cottage) to minimize its carbon footprint, I will invent a super weapon that Lance will use to destroy the monster in a final climactic battle in the end, from which he will emerge blackened and bloody and with his shirt torn off to display his gorgeous pecs and biceps."

I sighed. "It's no use," I said. "The Author has other plans for us."

"How can you say that, dahling!"

"Oh, you don't really mean that, Lance!"

"Don't ye be givin' up, matey!"

"Polly wants a cracker!"

"No," I said, "it is truly no use. As you know, Bob, the monster comes ashore from the ocean."

"Aye, matey."

"And it's a zombie, which as you know is a reanimated dead body."

"Aye…?"

I shrugged my shoulders and sat back to await my fate in the rocking chair. "There you have it. No one can ever defeat the marine corpse."

Author's Note

Michael Flynn is best known for the Hugo-nominated *Eifelheim* and the far-future Spiral Arm series. His short fiction has appeared in *Analog*, *Asimov's*, *F&SF*, and elsewhere. He has received the Sturgeon prize for his story "House of Dreams," and was the first recipient of the Robert A. Heinlein Award, for his body of work. In addition, he has received the Seiun Award from Japan and the Prix Julia-Verlanger from France, both for translations of *Eifelheim*.

He has been a Hugo finalist several times. He is currently working on a story series, The Journeyman, set in the Spiral Arm, and a novel, *The Shipwrecks of Time*, set in the alien world of 1965 Milwaukee.

Throw Me a Bone

Stanley Schmidt

The bone that became the bane of Bill Billingsley's existence was not the biggest ever found, nor was it a new species. He'd had hopes for both when he literally stumbled across it in the Patagonian high desert. The encounter reminded him of a documentary he'd once seen about the discovery of the enormous thighbone of the biggest Titanosaur yet found, and for one brief shining moment he'd hoped to surpass it in size, novelty, or both. But it was not to be. After titanic effort to excavate, prepare, and identify it, it had proved to be just another Titanosaur, of a species already well known to science. It was also well below record size, though it was bigger than Bill, and in life would have inspired far more shock and awe than anything now alive.

To add insult to injury, it was the *only* bone he found at the site. He exhausted his grant—and made a serious dent in his retirement fund—excavating a sizable chunk of land surrounding it. Not only did he find not a single bone that looked like a possible part of the same creature, he found no fossils at all. In the unanimous opinion of peer reviewers, those peculiar circumstances screamed "Fraud!" even though nobody denied that all the tests unequivocally proved that it was a thoroughly authentic Titanosaur bone. It just wasn't, they said, a Titanosaur that had met a natural demise in this spot. To them, that strongly suggested that Bill had tried to perpetrate an elaborate but embarrassingly naïve hoax, somehow acquiring a fossil bone elsewhere, planting it here, and expecting them to believe it was a new find even though it had none of the corroborating fragments that should have been nearby.

Needless to say, that drove Bill's career in paleontology into extinction—and that hurt. He knew his discovery was honest and real, and he was as perplexed as anybody that there was none of the context he would have expected. He would have been happy to spend the next twenty years trying to find out why, but nobody would even read his grant proposals anymore. And he couldn't dip further into his retirement money;

he was going to need that for retirement—though in effect, he was already far more retired than he'd ever hoped to be at his young age.

Disillusioned and embittered, he coasted for a while on savings, becoming a recluse in his own home. He tried for new jobs in academia and research labs, but they wouldn't even let him sweep floors. Eventually, desperate for a way to keep making ends meet, he wound up bagging groceries and hoping nobody would recognize him.

He wasn't sure whether to be disappointed or relieved that nobody did.

Until one fine spring day when he kept looking out the window and wishing he were there instead of at Register 6, and a distinguished-looking man he didn't recognize came through his lane and put a single package of buns and two cans of sardines on the belt. He rang the order up quickly, and almost dropped the bag he was filling when the man said, "It's a pleasure to meet you, Dr. Billingsley. Could I have a word with you at your next break?"

"You know me?" Bill said incredulously.

"I know *of* you, and I'd like to offer you a job. In paleontology."

Part of Bill was more excited than he'd been in a long time, while another part cautioned that whatever this guy was selling, it probably *was* as fraudulent as people had accused his work of being. Nonetheless, he agreed to talk for ten minutes at his break, which was coming up in twenty.

"My name is Cornell Jackson," the man said as they walked out to the corner of the building where the smokers took breaks. Bill stopped a discreet distance from them and gave "Jackson" his full attention. If he really was who he claimed, he'd been one of Bill's professional idols for a long time.

"It's an honor to meet you, sir. I've often wanted to ask you something about your work in Wyoming…"

A couple of simple questions convinced Bill that Jackson was for real, and Bill really was honored. "But why," he asked, "did you hunt me down here? I thought I was forever disgraced, and nobody in the field wanted anything to do with me."

"I do," said Jackson. "I always thought your work on your Titanosaur bone was impeccable, and the fact that you didn't find anything else near it was a genuine mystery that needed more investigation. So I went back to your site to poke around some more myself."

Bill smiled. "Well, I appreciate that, but I would have advised you against it. That way lies professional ruin."

Jackson returned the smile. "I realized that, but I was willing to risk it." He winked. "Besides, I found another pretext to work there without ever mentioning your name. I wangled enough money to do a lot more digging, farther from your bone site than you got before your money ran out. And you'll never guess what I found."

"Nothing?"

"*Au contraire.*" He produced a smartphone and showed Bill a series of stunning pictures.

Bill looked at them with a deepening frown. "That looks like some sort of... village," he said finally.

"Exactly," said Jackson. "But look at this one."

It was just like the one before it: a group of structures in an excavated pit that looked like some unfamiliar sort of huts or shacks. But Jackson was standing next to them, looking like a tiny action figure.

Bill felt his heart pounding as he put it together. "A settlement," he said under his breath, "of really huge prehistoric beings? Probably reptilian?"

"Exactly," Jackson repeated, grinning. He switched to another picture. "This is an artist's conception of what we think they may have looked like. Cool, no?"

"Way beyond cool," Bill agreed. "But what does it have to do with me?"

"There's an awful lot to learn there," said Jackson. "And I want you to help us learn about it. If anybody on Earth has a right to be in on this, you do."

Bill frowned. "And why is that?"

"Well, look at this." Jackson switched to one more picture, showing another huge creature, a bit smaller than the others, and decidedly different in build. "You remember that bone you found?"

Bill winced. "How could I forget?"

"Well, Bill... this is the dog that buried it."

Author's Note

Stanley Schmidt was editor of *Analog Science Fiction and Fact* for 34 years, but was writing for it before that and is now at it again, having retired from editing and headed for the hills (literally). Every story in this book can be read in one sitting; this one was also written in one sitting, immediately after watching the documentary referenced near the beginning.

Relatively Speaking

Darrell Schweitzer and Lee Weinstein

Susan Kendall hurried through the crowded lobby of the Bethair Institute for Biomedical Research. She swerved to avoid an Asian woman wearing a feminist insignia who was talking to a reporter and nearly collided with a black couple carrying placards. She took the stairs to the second floor, pushed open the door marked DIRECTOR, and found her fiancé, Dr. Jeffrey Barker, pacing the laboratory floor nervously.

"Jeff, what is going on down there? It looks like the UN is having a confrontation in the lobby."

"No, it's a madhouse. A genuine madhouse. Reverend Sun plans to send over a busload of his people, and there's the Vegetarian Congress, and Pope George Ringo sent an emissary. In twenty minutes I am going to have to address that mob in the meeting room. Out of the thousands of applications that have gotten through the *first* screening, I have to pick the first human subject to be cloned. Whoever I choose will go down in history. No matter who I pick, I will be attacked for favoritism. Every minority, every majority, every *every*body wants the honor. And then there is the press to deal with. How do I decide?"

She pulled out a stool and sat down. "Once the first one takes, the others should follow very closely. They'll all be 'first' in a sense."

"I'm sure the second man to fly the Atlantic solo followed 'very closely.' But can anyone remember his name?"

"I see. Have you checked their genetic backgrounds?"

"Yes, and they're all as perfect as human beings can be. I could draw a name out of a hat, but a lot of them aren't going to sit still and be passed over because of the vagaries of chance. If only I had some solid objective criterion to work from."

He sat down wearily on another stool, and both were silent for a moment. Then she spoke.

"Maybe you are approaching it wrong. This is an added luxury, right? All those people can have babies in the ordinary way, maybe even identical twins, which are nothing but natural clones in the first place. What about someone who can't? It's like deciding who gets a second helping when a lot of people haven't been fed yet."

"*That's it!*" he exclaimed, brushing a heap of papers off a desk into a wastebasket. "Sue, you have saved my day."

"I did?" she said as she followed him out.

A dozen flashbulbs went off as Dr. Barker walked into the meeting room. On cue, he went to the front of the room, took the microphone, and waited for quiet.

"In a few minutes," he said, "I'll give you a short history of this project. But before that, I should like to explain how the volunteer to provide the genetic material for the first attempt at human cloning will be chosen. I have given this a great deal of thought, and I believe I have come up with an equitable solution." He cleared his throat. A murmur rose from the crowd, then died down.

"The real credit should go to my fiancée, Miss Sue Kendall, who gave me the added insight I needed. The subject for the experiment will be chosen on the basis of two things: first, contrary to those out there who would have us believe that scientists are as unfeeling as the glass in their test tubes, we are interested in the welfare of the child. The first clone baby will have unprecedented problems in adjustment. Therefore we need someone who can devote his or her full time to the upbringing of the clone. An institutional, or large family situation, in which the child might be neglected or overshadowed by others, is obviously not desirable. Secondly, there's the matter of who *needs* cloning instead of who *wants* it for the novelty. I think most of you are capable of having children in the time-honored fashion."

He paused while the snickering subsided, then continued.

"The first 'parent' of a clone must be someone who is genetically sound, but incapable of having offspring, either because of age or accidental sterilization. And it should be someone who has no living relative and needs this child of science to continue their line. And so, ladies and gentlemen, I thought it only fair that he among you who is without kin grow the first clone."

Authors' Note

Darrell Schweitzer has a strong leaning to the dark side (dark fantasy and horror). He is also a critic, essayist, and anthologist. His most recent book is *The Threshold of Forever: Essays and Reviews* (Wildside, 2017).

Lee Weinstein is a retired Philadelphia librarian who writes more reviews and essays than fiction.

Our Wonderful Kickstarter Supporters:

A Proud Supporter
Alvin Helms (Graphic Artist & Designer)
Andrew Greengrass
Andrew Hatchell
anonymous
anonymous
Anouk Arnal
Athaclena
Author Bud Sparhawk
Aysha Rehm
Bennett
Beth Lobdell
Bill Clawson
Bruce Berger
Carol Gyzander
Cathy Green
Chad Bowden
Danielle Ackley-McPhail
Darsey Meredith
Dave Bush
David Kowal
DejaBobbi
Dennis Higbee
Dominic
Emily Henderson
Emily Williams
Eric Frank
G.E. Robertson
George Macoukji
Hamish Perpetual Brookeman
Hiram G Wells
Ian Harvey
Ian Law
James McKelvey
Jamieson Cobleigh
Jan
Jaq Greenspon
Jay V. Schindler
Jonathan A. Gillett
Jonathan Baker

Josh Prober
Josh Rosenthal
Kevin Lauderdale
Kevin Lee
King of His Domain
Kristin Janz
Leigh
Lisa Padol
Liv Smith
Mark Grasdal
Mark Lukens
Mayer Brenner
Melissa Wright
Michael A. Burstein
Michael M. Jones
MJ Kelleher
M.S. Spray
Oliver D. Dickerson III
Olivia Johnston
Pam Nemeth
Pat Bellavance
Patricia Hayes
Rachel Bitterfield
Randee Dawn
Rhel
Ron and Elizabeth Howard
Ronen Friedman
Samuel Aronoff
Sean Guerino
Sharan Volin
Soh Kam Yung
Stefan Hull
SwordFire
Tasha Turner
Thanks Tana! Fire Chicks Rock!
Thomas Colwell
Thomas Donaghey
Throne Sitter Paul Hess (@idea2go)
Tom Easton
W.A. Brown

CPSIA information can be obtained
at www.ICGtesting.com
Printed in the USA
FSOW01n2122060717
36091FS